WINNING
EVERY DAY

WINNING EVERY DAY

gold medal advice for a happy, healthy life!

BY GYMNASTICS GOLD MEDALIST
SHANNON MILLER

with Nancy Ann Richardson

bantam books

new york • toronto • london • sydney • auckland

Published by
Bantam Books
Bantam Doubleday Dell Publishing Group, Inc.
1540 Broadway
New York, New York 10036

Bantam Books are published by Bantam Books, a division of Bantam Doubleday Dell Publishing Group, Inc. Its trademark, consisting of the words "Bantam Books" and the portrayal of a rooster, is Registered in U.S. Patent and Trademark Office and in other countries. Marca Registrada.

Library of Congress Cataloging-in-Publication Data
Miller, Shannon.
Winning every day : gold medal advice for a happy, healthy life! /
by Shannon Miller with Nancy Ann Richardson.
p.   cm.
ISBN 0-553-09776-8
1. Miller, Shannon, 1977–   —Juvenile literature.   2. Gymnasts—
United States—Biography—Juvenile literature.   I. Richardson,
Nancy Ann.   II. Title.
GV460.2.M55A3   1998
796.44'092—dc21
[B] 98—10059
CIP

The text of this book is set in 13-point Adobe Garamond.

Book design by Susan Clark
Manufactured in the United States of America
June 1998
10 9 8 7 6 5 4 3 2 1

contents

© 1997 Frank Veronsky

introduction

Winning is all it's cracked up to be. However, the process of getting there is highly underrated. It's the challenges, tough times, and even the defeats that form the stepping-stones to the top. Motivation, discipline, faith, and the day-to-day job of taking care of yourself the best way you can aren't just part of the process of winning—they're what makes you a winner, whether or not you stand on an Olympic podium with a gold medal around your neck.

Personal character gets built along the way, not at the moment you score a perfect 10. And if you work on who you are and who you want to be, as well as decide what you want to accomplish in school, sports, jobs, or relationships, and set realistic goals to get yourself there, you'll be winning every day!

This book is dedicated to my family, coaches, friends, and fans. They've all given me so much love and support, and now it's my turn to give something back by sharing how I succeeded in being a winner both inside and outside the gym. I believe that the things I've learned in the past twenty-one years can help other people. The following pages are filled with diary entries, competition and personal stories, and golden rules passed down from my mother to me. I hope they show that anything worthwhile takes hard work and determination . . . and that it's worth the effort.

Sincerely,

The beginning of the dream . . .

gymnastics

November 1993

Dear Diary,

Today I came home from Steve's annual picnic for his gymnasts and told my parents that I want to quit gymnastics. Mom and Dad didn't act surprised, they just asked why. Considering how supportive they've been throughout my career, I definitely owed them an answer. I told them how my back is really hurting from the pounding of practice. The pain is only temporary—it's because I've been growing a lot—but it makes me wonder if I'm still happy in the sport I've loved since I was five years old.

My parents and I talked for a long time. I said that I felt like I'd reached the end of my career. I mean, I went to the 1992 Barcelona Olympics and won five medals. That's more right there than I ever dreamed of doing—and more than any other U.S. athlete! And last month I won three gold medals, including the gold for all-around, at my first World Championships in Birmingham, England. What else is there?

I wasn't sure if there was anything else, but before I made such a big decision Mom and Dad wanted me to talk to Steve. "We just want to make sure this is what you want," they told me. And they both assured me they're 100 percent behind my decision, whatever it turns out to be.

My parents called Steve, and he came over to the house. Steve, my parents, and I all sat down at our dining room table, and I told him I was thinking about quitting. The first thing Steve asked me was, "What are your goals?" I kind of laughed, remembering how Steve used to make me, and all the gymnasts he coaches, fill out goal cards. We'd write down new skills we wanted to learn on bars, beam, floor, and vault. And then we'd set about learning each one. That seems like a while ago now. For the past few years, I've mostly focused on doing well in big competitions, polishing everyday skills and working on tougher ones. "What are your goals?" Steve repeated. And that's when I knew that the problem isn't the pain in my back, or that I want to leave gymnastics. It's that I don't have anything to look forward to. I'm bored. I need something new.

Steve told me that there are lots of things I've never done before. I've never been to the Goodwill Games, or won two consecutive all-around titles at the World Championships—no American ever has. I've never even considered the possibility that I could go to another Olympics, since most people think I'll be too old by 1996. Can you believe nineteen is considered an old lady in gymnastics?

Steve said that anything is possible, and I believe him. "But what about my back?" I asked. We decided that we'll start using the more cushioned tumble tracks for practices, and that I'll begin a different training schedule. Up until today, I've been working out with the younger kids in the gym—you know, the thirteen-year-olds who are still putting in their time. I've already done the kind of training where each beam, bar, and floor routine is practiced twelve times in a row. I don't need that type of repetition anymore. Steve and I can step back a little bit, work on some new skills, and not take as hard a pounding. He said cutting back will not only help me improve, but will prolong my career. When Steve left, I felt like a weight had been lifted off my shoulders!

I'm pretty relieved that I'm not quitting. I've always needed goals to get motivated, and now I have new ones. I'm going to try to make the Goodwill team, and compete in other competitions I've never attended. There are a lot of skills I haven't perfected, and ones that haven't even been dreamed up yet! But the Olympics in '96? I think Steve might be pushing it there. Still, who knows . . .

• why gymnastics? •

In the beginning, the answer to that question was simple. I loved gymnastics. Looking back now, the answer is different. I love gymnastics because of the person it's helped me to be. It's been the training, competing, losing, and winning that have made me a strong, motivated, goal-oriented, disciplined young woman. I see now that the more I gave to the sport, the better person I became. It's been a thrilling and sometimes difficult process. Since I'm only twenty-one years old, it's far from over, but I wouldn't trade a single moment.

Gymnastics has never been about winning, at least not for me. It's about that feeling of floating through the air, that moment of sticking a perfect landing, the excitement of learning new skills, and the sense of ac-

Flying through the air at my gym in Oklahoma.
© *Dave Black 1998*

complishment that comes from hard work. And gymnastics is hard work, even for me. Sure, I have some natural ability. But success comes from putting in the time and the effort. I think that's true of anything.

I've always been a perfectionist. When I was a little kid, I'd spend hours on the uneven bars trying to learn new skills. The first big one I got was a giant—a full swing around the high bar. The rest of the gymnasts had left for the day, and my mom was talking to my coach. After probably more than a thousand failed attempts and falls, I made one giant. It was an incredible feeling. And even though my coach had spent months teaching me the technique, I realized *I* was the one who'd pushed myself to stay late, to do better.

• my early history •

A lot of people think that from the moment I could walk, I was tumbling in the gym. That's just not true! My older sister, Tessa, and I started taking dance lessons when I was about four years old. We got bored pretty fast, so we begged my parents for a trampoline for Christmas. Pretty soon we were bouncing, flipping, and twisting. My parents thought we were going to fly off the trampoline and kill ourselves, so they enrolled us both in a noncompetitive recreational gymnastics program in Edmond, Oklahoma, my hometown.

From the start I loved gymnastics. But I only went to the club, Adventures in Gymnastics, a few times a week. And I never became obsessed with gymnastics. In fact, I watched tons of TV as a kid, but never watched gymnastics. I've seen a few highlight tapes of Nadia Comaneci, and my coach, Steve Nunno, sometimes does video analyses of his gymnasts, but other than that, I still don't enjoy watching gymnastics. It make me too antsy—I just can't sit still that long. I watch my friends compete and that's fun, but I'd rather be out there doing it than in the stands.

Tessa liked gymnastics, but she never loved it. After a few months at Adventures in Gymnastics, my sister decided she wanted to be a swimmer—and she also wanted to take art lessons. I stayed at the gym. People always ask me if my sister is sorry she dropped out, or if there's some sort of weird competition between us because I succeeded in the sport. I have to laugh when I hear that. Tessa's finished college and she's going to medical school. Between our childhood and now, she's done everything—horseback riding, swimming, cross-country running, and rock climbing, to name a few. I'm just as proud of her as she is of me. There's a good lesson in that—you have to follow your own dreams, not someone else's.

When the coach at Adventures in Gymnastics asked my parents if I could come in to train a few more times a week, they weren't sure it was a good idea. They thought I was going to get tired of gymnastics. But my dad, a college professor, had time between classes, and he offered to drive me to the gym for as long as I wanted to go. He asked me to tell him if I got tired of it, and we'd stop. I don't think he could've guessed that I'd never get tired of it, or that there would never be anything I didn't like about the sport!

• the events •

Today the media always ask, "What's your favorite part of the sport?" I tell them I've never had a favorite event, and I enjoy them all. Maybe I enjoy beam a little more than the rest, but that distinction didn't happen until the media made me think about it. The truth is that I don't think in terms of most or least favorite, or best or worst event, because I don't want to get it in my head that I don't like one event. As soon as that happens I'll start worrying and that will affect both my individual-event and overall performance.

So, having said I like all the events, I can admit that as a little kid I was most attracted to the beam. A lot of gymnasts don't like beam because there's not much room for error. But that really appeals to the perfectionist in me. Years later, when I started training with Peggy Liddick (she's been my beam coach and floor choreographer since 1988), I began to understand why I love beam so much.

Math, physics, and geometry have always been my favorite subjects, and Peggy looks at the beam and different skills in terms of angles and degrees. She has always been able to explain why moving my arm or changing an angle will help me stay on the beam. When I can understand how to move individual body parts, I can learn new skills more easily. Most young gymnasts just think about staying on the beam, but the process is more important to me, and when I understand things, I can improve.

Of course, in the beginning it was all about actually staying *on* the beam. The first series I ever learned on the beam was a gainer back handspring, back handspring, back handspring. It was cool, because most of the kids in my gym weren't doing three in a row. I also did a double twisting dismount, which at a young age is considered a hard skill. A lot of beginning gymnasts are afraid of dismounts, because if you miss your feet at the end of the beam, or you're crooked going into it, you can hurt yourself. I was so young that I didn't know about fear yet.

• fear and pain •

So what about fear? Gymnastics is a lot like life. Everyone gets scared, and everyone falls. The key is to get right back up and try again. My coaches have always been really good about that, because if you fall and don't try again, the fear begins to build. And once fear has the chance to settle in, it takes a long time to get over it and back on track again.

As for the pain of falling, hitting the beam, or missing a skill . . . well, there's pain in any sport. That's just the way it is. I've pulled hamstrings, which can be pretty painful, and my back began to ache after the 1993 World Championships. But the ache eventually stopped because I took care of myself. Just like fear, pain shouldn't be ignored. It should be understood and dealt with.

• gymnastics lessons = life lessons •

Fear and pain aren't the only things that gymnastics has taught me about life. When I was only nine years old, I learned my first big lesson—if you want something badly enough, you can make it happen. In 1986 my coach at Adventures told his five top gymnasts (I was one of them) about a very exciting opportunity: a trip to the Soviet Union. The gyms in Moscow had always been very secretive and closed to the outside world. This was the first time that American gymnasts were going to be allowed in to train with the Russian coaches and their gymnasts. The training camp would be two weeks long; the gymnasts would train while the coaches would learn new techniques.

Of course everybody wanted to go, but we didn't have enough money to make the trip. Our coach and parents suggested we hold fund-raisers and have gymnastics shows to make money. We threw ourselves into the task and, because of lots of hard work and the generosity of our local community, raised enough money for all of us to go over! I remember flying to Russia and feeling very proud. I'd wanted this so badly and our hard work had made it happen.

• steve and me •

As it turned out, that trip to Moscow changed my life. I loved the Russian coaches. They were really nice and I had a lot of fun. They helped me work on some of the bigger skills. There was only one problem. I wanted to do each new skill so perfectly that if I couldn't figure one out, I'd start to cry. I wasn't sad, I was just unbelievably frustrated. I wanted to learn everything the Russian coaches could teach me, but I wasn't technically trained or prepared for the big skills.

My mom, who had come on the trip with me, saw my frustration and went to talk to an American who was in Moscow for the coaching seminar. His name was Steve Nunno and he coached in Norman, Oklahoma. Steve was a former National Collegiate All-Around performer at the University of Massachusetts, with degrees in business administration and sports administration. He'd coached with Bela Karolyi in Texas, and had moved to Oklahoma to assist in coaching the women's team at the University of Oklahoma. He had recently established the Dynamo Team Program in Oklahoma.

Steve told my mom that I had potential. He said he could see just how intensely I wanted to do well, but that the crying was taking too much energy out of me. I wasn't ready for the high-level skills the Russians were trying to teach

I loved being in Russia!

me, but Steve thought that with the right training, one day I might be.

When we returned to the United States, my mom called Steve. She told him that I'd learned all I could at Adventures in Gymnastics. I was ready for the next level, and because my gym didn't have a competitive team and I wanted to be able to compete, we'd decided to look for a new coach. Mom asked if I could try out at Dynamo Gymnastics, his training center in Norman, which was about a forty-five-minute drive from our house. Steve said yes.

Walking into Dynamo was like entering a new world. In my old gym, I'd been the best gymnast. At Steve's, there were older girls doing big skills. I was in awe! At the time, Steve was renting space in Bart Connor's gym. There were only ten or twelve girls, and we all trained together. That meant I could watch the better girls work out, which was a huge encouragement for me. As far as coaching goes, Steve was a great motivator. I really lucked out with him, because I was only nine years old and I had no idea what to look for in a coach.

• what you need to succeed
(at any level) •

When you're just starting in a sport, it's hard to know what you need. Here are the top ten things I think any kid should look for in a gymnastics coach.

1. A good motivator—your coach has to know what makes you tick, excel, and thrive.
2. Someone very knowledgeable about gymnastics and good technique.
3. Someone safety-certified who knows how to spot.
4. A good, honest, and kind person.
5. Someone who understands *The Code of Points* (that's the little green book that lists all the gymnastics skills, what they're worth, and how many of each type you need in each routine). Not understanding this can start a routine at a 9.6 instead of a 10 and can lose a competition for a gymnast before it even starts.
6. Someone you can listen to and understand. You can't make improvements and corrections if you don't understand your coach.
7. A coach, not a friend. You're not paying for a friend.
8. Someone you respect.
9. Someone who believes in good nutrition.
10. Someone who makes gymnastics fun—because if it's not fun, you shouldn't be doing it!

• you don't just take from gymnastics, it gives back •

Home from Atlanta with the gold.
© *Garrison Photography—Edmond*

If you know what to look for in a coach, you're on the right track. But gymnastics, at least for me, hasn't only been about finding the right coach and having him or her work with me. I've gotten so much more out of the sport. The obvious things are flexibility, strength, and good nutrition. But it's also given me goals and direction. And the discipline I've learned has carried through into schoolwork, given me a way to budget my time, and helped me develop a sense of pride and self-worth.

I'm not just Shannon Miller, Olympic champion. That title only tells you what I've accomplished in the sport. It's what brought me to that point, what I learned along the way, that really matters. Because all that I've

11

learned is going to stay with me long after I step off the podium and take that gold medal from around my neck.

I remember my first state competition. I was ten years old, class two. As I walked into the gym, I was pretty nervous. I'd only been in a few other competitions—mostly intersquad ones that Steve set up to get his gymnasts ready for competition. In those meets, once I got into the arena I was fine and my nerves settled. But this competition was big. My first event was the beam. I did a back handspring layout stepout and fell off the beam.

I could have been crushed. And maybe if I hadn't spent a year with Steve before States, I would have been. But Steve had been drilling it into my head that everyone made mistakes and there was nothing to do when you made one but learn from it and move on. So I told myself it was just a mistake and that I was trying my best. Then I climbed back onto the beam and finished my routine.

I continued to try my best through the competition, and when it was over I'd won! But even if I hadn't won it wouldn't have mattered in the grand scheme of things. Because the kid who'd been crying hysterically in Russia just a year before was slowly being replaced by one who understood that the only thing that mattered about a mistake was whether or not you took the opportunity to learn from it.

The wisdom I've learned in gymnastics affects every part of my life. I used to get devastated if I did something wrong. Now I look at things differently. If I do poorly on a college exam and I've tried my best, I don't dwell on the grade. I just try to figure out how to do better the next time. I'll study twice as hard or do extra-credit work. If I have a fight with my parents or a friend, I try to understand what happened, solve the difficulty, and move forward. Sometimes it's not easy, but it's part of life. And it's not the mistakes you make that matter, it's what you do about them.

Shannon's Advice for Young Gymnasts: Don't go into the sport thinking you're going to make the Olympic team. There are only seven spots and millions of gymnasts with an eye on them. Go into the sport because you have fun doing it, not because of "what ifs" and dreams of a gold medal. That way, no matter what happens, you win.

Shannon's Golden Rule: Fear = False Evidence Appearing Real. Have no fear!

(My mom writes sayings on index cards and gives them to me to take to competitions. I look at a new one each day, and they give me strength. I've ended each chapter of this book with one of these special golden rules of inspiration.)

motivation

June 1996

Dear Diary,

Maybe Steve is right—I'm best as an underdog. When a competition is going really smoothly and there's no adversity, I'm not quite as motivated. But when I have to dig myself out of a tough spot, I always fight harder. And that's what happened today at U.S. Nationals. You know how I love the beam? Well, it was my first event at the competition and I was really ready to get out there and perform. I guess I wasn't focused enough as I stepped onto the podium and prepared for my press mount. At that moment I never could've imagined what was going to happen next.

There's no room for big mistakes on the beam. The unthinkable happened halfway through my routine: I fell off on my layout series. I was really disappointed, but I climbed back on and finished my routine. When I hit my landing, I raised my arms and saluted the judges. I felt like the smile on my face was like those fake buildings they use for sets in Western movies . . . paper thin and empty.

I walked back over to my gym bag and sat down. I didn't want to make eye contact with my coach. I knew in the back of my mind that I had to get over the fall and focus on the next three events, but I felt numb. I wasn't in tears or anything, I just felt like all of my energy had been drained. Like my limbs were heavy as lead and hollow. Part of me didn't feel like even bothering to finish the competition, and another part knew I had to keep competing. I was stuck somewhere in the middle of those two thoughts. In limbo.

Steve saw the look on my face and came over to me. He put his hands on my shoulders and looked me straight in the eye. "Okay, we've got to get going now," he said.

That's it. Just that one sentence. But I've been with him for eleven years now, and I can almost read his mind. I knew exactly what Steve was saying: "It's time to get motivated, Shannon. Shake off the memory of the beam and look forward. Remember that the biggest mistake of all is letting a mistake get the best of you."

Steve and I walked over to the floor and he stretched me out so I'd be loose for my next routine. He started to get excited (he always does) as he went over all of my corrections—reminding me to block hard off the floor, keep my arms straight, stick my landings, and really perform my dance. His excitement was catching, and by the time I was called onto the floor I'd forgotten all about the beam. I just wanted to get out there and show myself and everyone else what I was capable of doing!

I won the all-around, but even though the gold medal was great, it's not what I'm most proud of accomplishing. When the going got tough, I pulled myself together, and Steve was the one who helped me to do that by reminding me of who I am and what I can do. It was our combined effort that won the gold today.

Focusing on doing my best at the '96 Nationals.
© *Dave Black 1998*

Yet in the end it's all up to me, isn't it? As much as I depend on Steve and Peggy and my parents, sister, brother, and friends, I guess the bottom line is that I have to be my own motivator, judge, and jury. And if I try my best, there's no way I can lose.

• motivation and me •

I have always been my own number-one motivator. I think that's because I want to do everything faultlessly—that includes school, appearances, and charity work, as well as gymnastics. That's just the perfectionist in me coming out again. I've been able to motivate myself to be in shape, to work out, and to do well or at least try to do well at everything I set my mind to. So how do I do it? Here's a list of seven things that help me get motivated. Maybe they'll work for you, too!

Jessica and Barbara Davis, me, Kim Zmeskal, and Kim's boyfriend, Chris Burdette, rocking to the Rolling Stones in San Francisco!

1. Music, music, music. I love country and Top 40, especially Garth Brooks and groups like Hanson and Sister Hazel. Whatever I listen to has to have a loud, upbeat rhythm to get me going.
2. Breaking the monotony. If I change a pattern—studying at a dif-

Taking a night off in Atlanta during the 1996 John Hancock Tour with good friends Amanda Borden and John Macready.

ferent time, riding my bike to classes instead of driving, or training a different way—the change helps to motivate me.

3. Learning something new. I love taking different classes, learning a new recreational sport (my latest is figure skating), or practicing a new gymnastics skill. If you're not learning, life gets pretty stagnant and boring.

4. Remembering how good something feels once I've completed it. I hate to go running, but if I can recall how great I feel when it's over, it helps me put on my sneakers and hit the pavement.

5. Spending time with friends. Working out together, seeing a movie, studying—being with my friends gets me motivated.

6. Keeping things fun. That's the real secret to motivation—if an activity is fun, you want to do it!

7. Talking to friends and family. Sometimes it helps to talk about things, the way I did with Steve in 1993, when I was thinking about

quitting gymnastics. People who care about you can give you perspective on a situation and help you find motivation.

• motivation and coaches (peggy and steve) •

I'm lucky to have gymnastics coaches like Steve and Peggy to help motivate me. Peggy is amazing. She has really high expectations for me, and every day I'm in the gym, I want to live up to them. Peggy always puts 100 percent of her time and effort into coaching me, so I want to do well for both of us.

Steve is really good about getting me going, too. If he has early-morning practices for his gymnasts, he always blasts really loud music to pump us up. He switches our routine around so each practice isn't the same—which is key if you spend six to eight hours in the gym every day. For example, instead of doing typical conditioning exercises, like run-

My coaches. *Courtesy of Shade Global*

ning and jumping, he'll have us race sprints or work with a partner on lunges and calf raises. Sometimes, when he knows his gymnasts are getting bored, he'll pull out *The Code of Points* and say, "Pick out whatever you want to learn today." That gives us some control over our practice and gets us excited.

Of course, when elite gymnasts are preparing for a major competition, there's no time for piggyback rides or games. It's not hard to get motivated when something like the World Championships or the Olympics is in sight. In fact, I think competitions on that level are the biggest motivator of all—at least for me. But still, it helps to have a coach who can lighten things up a bit.

The 1996 training camp for the U.S. Olympic women's gymnastics team was held two weeks before the Olympics in Greenville, South Carolina. Each day brought us closer and closer to July 18, 1996, and the 1996 Olympics. Instead of staying in the Olympic Village, our entire team was

Steve giving me some advice during the 1996 Olympic warm-ups. *Photo by Gene Stafford*

19

secluded in a fraternity house on the Emory University campus near Atlanta's Georgia Dome. The media had surrounded the place, and even though it was quiet and comfortable inside the house, we still knew that outside there was a lot of chaos. Steve understood the pressure, and he knew that we were all getting tired, sore, and a bit bored with our training. So he made sure to play great music to get us going, and he tried to make us laugh when he could.

Sometimes being a great motivator means figuring out what people need. For a coach, it can involve lightening the mood, or it can involve yelling at a gymnast who needs a verbal kick in the butt to get her going. Steve has done both for me, and the key has always been knowing when I need each one. He knows me so well that he understands the times I need to be joked with and when he has to react more strongly. That's what makes him a great coach and the perfect motivational force for me. It's funny, but I usually know when the yelling is coming. It always happens when I'm feeling blah, and more often than not, I'm waiting for Steve to do something about it.

• motivational movers and shakers •

The truth is that even if you have a coach to motivate you, that relationship isn't going to last forever. And coaches don't touch every aspect of your life, anyway. Sure, there are parents, siblings, teachers, and friends, but counting on them to motivate you isn't fair. They've all got their own lives, and while they might be able to help you out, if you can motivate yourself, then you're golden. That doesn't mean that you can't look to other people, but it's important to know where the true responsibility for yourself lies.

My family has always played a part in my gymnastics career. After I became involved in the sport, my mom started judging. She understood the skills, degrees, and levels, and if I had any questions, she knew the answers. After practice she used to ask me how I'd done at the gym and what I was learning. I'd tell her about a tough skill and she'd give me incentives to learn it—like a Cabbage Patch doll or my choice for dinner that night. Mom had seen me stay late at practice to work on a skill too many times to believe that I truly needed this additional motivation. I would've tried to master those skills without the prizes, but it involved her in the learning process and made it even more fun and exciting. Dad, on the other hand, didn't know much about gymnastics. He just

wanted me to be happy and have fun. He's always been so great that way. If I wanted to be a gymnast, cool. If not, no big deal.

I never had the stereotypical gymnastics parents, though I would say that stereotype tends to be more the thing of movies than real life. My parents hardly ever came to watch my practices because they both have full-time jobs. My dad is chairman of the physics department at the University of Central Oklahoma and my mom is a vice president of the First National Bank of Edmond. There was just no way they could sit and

My parents joined me at the 1997 Babe Zaharias awards.

watch me for hours on end. Plus, most meets were out of state, and quite costly to attend. But they drove me to practices and always had time to listen. I think that's why I've had such great experiences in gymnastics. I do it because I love it, not because anyone ever pushed me. I'm pretty stubborn. There's no way someone could just tell me to do something, because that's a sure way to get me not to do it! The bottom line is that I'm my own motivational force and I wouldn't have it any other way.

• the hometown advantage •

Edmond, Oklahoma, has been my hometown for over eighteen years now. I love living there for so many reasons: the fresh air, the country atmosphere, and most of all the warm and friendly people who are always willing to lend a hand to help someone out. I loved growing up in a place that looked and felt like the country—right down to the wheat fields and cow pastures!—but that also had the conveniences of the city right there as well.

The people of Edmond have always been very supportive of me. Before the 1992 Olympics, they helped raise money for my family to travel to Barcelona and see me compete. After the Olympics, I came home to a parade given in my honor as well as that of my family and coaches. The parade alone was a huge thrill—but at the end, one of Edmond's local car dealerships presented me with a red Saturn! I was really excited about that! The support I received from the people of Edmond continued over the next four years, and after the 1996 Olympics, they had another parade . . . and another dealership traded me my Saturn for a hunter green Camaro! But while the cars and parades were truly great, it's the Oklahoman people themselves who have always helped mo-

Saying hi to the hometown fans.

tivate me: Their generosity of spirit and Southwestern amiability is something I've grown to appreciate more and more. I really love traveling all over the world, but it's always good to have a place like Oklahoma to call home.

I still can't believe I have my own billboard!

Shannon's Advice: Love what you do, do what you love. Be your own motivator and you can accomplish anything you set your mind to.

Shannon's Golden Rule: Hold on to the enduring, the good, and the true, and you will bring these into your experience.

setting goals

August 1997

Dear Diary,

Sorry I haven't written in a while, but the past two weeks have been crazy! It started when I decided at the last minute to train for the World University Games taking place in Catania, Italy. Steve made the suggestion only a few weeks before trials began, and even though I wasn't sure I was eligible, or if I had enough time to get into shape, we started to train. It turned out I was eligible and in good enough shape to make the team. I was excited because the World University Games were something I'd never done before!

Since I hadn't been training very hard, I knew I had to step up my practices or else I wouldn't do well at the Games. It was hard, however, because I was still traveling an average of four days a week. That meant the time I did get to spend in the gym had to count. Finding time is tough when you've got thirty-six hours of commitments and only twenty-four hours to do them!

My schedule, as usual, has been completely hectic! ABC was here all day Wednesday and Thursday to film a segment on me for a TV special. They tagged along to my parents' house, the gym, and my new apartment.

One of my biggest goals since the Olympic Games was to get my own apartment. I'm twenty years old, and it's time to start living independently. I love my family dearly and I see them a lot, but I wanted to move closer to the University of Oklahoma campus and to begin to be a part of things. I was tired of commuting to school, because I'd just drive there, take classes, and then drive to the gym to train or back home to Edmond. I wanted to ride my bike to classes, hang out with other students, and make new friends. I recently moved in—and I love it! It's nice to decorate your own place, although I don't have a lot of time to shop for furniture and stuff. But slowly it's starting to look like home. Having a film crew in my new place was fun but exhausting.

On Friday I raced out of practice for a two-hour Bank of Oklahoma appearance, then studied all night so I could pass a correspondence-course test I had to take on Saturday. I thought about putting the test off, but I couldn't think of a better time, so I buckled down and studied. On Sunday I flew to Cleveland to do a shoe store opening, then flew back the same day to work out at the gym.

The next morning I flew to New York City to work at Steve's gymnastics camp, Team USA, for a day, went to the Garth Brooks concert in Central Park (it was great and our location was unbeliev-

I'm a country girl at heart.

able!), and then back to Steve's camp the next day to do a clinic. Then I flew back home to Oklahoma, packed, and flew to Chicago for a two-day training camp for the World University Games. After that I flew to Denver for two more days of training and an award ceremony, and then on to Rome, Italy, for the competition.

If the flying part sounds easy, it wasn't. I almost missed my flight to Italy, and I had to do some pretty crazy nonstop flying and driving to catch the right plane out of

New York. Of course, the airline lost my luggage somewhere between Denver, New York, and Rome. I had my computer with me, but I couldn't do any work because my voltage converters were in my lost bag. Without a working modem, I couldn't fax or e-mail.

I thought about phoning my mom when I got to Rome and having her take care of some work stuff, but then decided against it. Not only did I make the decision to move out of my parents' house this year, I made the decision to take my career, finances, and professional obligations onto my own shoulders. When the going gets a little tough, I'm not just going to throw it back in my mom's lap.

In addition to my work things, I was also missing all my gymnastics stuff—leotards, warm-ups, hair ties—basically everything I needed for the competition. Luckily, the other U.S. gymnasts competing there and the coaches helped pull together everything I needed.

The competition was exciting, and different since the competitors are university students from around the world. I won the all-around and the team placed second. I was really pleased that I did so well on such short notice and after such a challenging few weeks.

Believe it or not, after telling you about the last few weeks and how hectic they were, I have to confess that I

Inside the Colosseum, Rome, 1997.

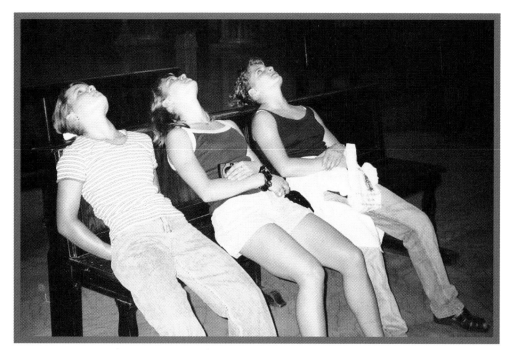

Checking out the amazing murals with gymnasts Kristi Lichey and Kathleen Shrieves.

could have written sooner. I mean, my bags arrived a few days after the competition ended (the team stayed in Italy for a vacation after the World University Games). So why didn't I write?

I can't really point to any one thing. It was the balcony attached to my hotel room that overlooked the water. And how beautiful Catania was in the late summer. It was the delicious food, and the quiet calm of no phone, no fax, and no computer. I had a few books I'd carried over in my shoulder bag, and after the competition was finished I curled up in a chair on the balcony and read. It sounds so simple, but I haven't been that relaxed in years!

Since moving out on my own and trying to balance all my new responsibilities, I haven't taken any time just for myself. When I look at my calendar, a typical day has me doing some type of appearance, having a conference call about my new book, flying to Atlanta for another appearance, and training and studying. That's all in one *day! A few days from now I'm flying to Los Angeles for a pediatric AIDS benefit, then to Dallas for a premiere, then back to L.A. the next morning for Tessa's graduation, then driving that night to Bakersfield to do a two-day gymnastics camp. Then I'm off to Phoenix for a new product launch, autograph signing, and shooting a commercial. Whew!*

I'm not complaining. Right now I'm in the fast lane and I love it! But those few days in Rome reminded me of something. I've got to make time for myself. Maybe it's just a weekend where I don't answer the phone or I read a book for fun. Or maybe it's just a few hours when I put my work aside and go for a walk or see a movie. Anyway, that's one of my new goals—making time for me. I'll add it to the list and see what I can do. . . .

Leah Brown, Kathleen Shrieves, me, and Kristi Lichey outside the Colosseum making friends with the Romans.

• getting started with goals •

I can't remember a time when I didn't set goals for myself. I'm a list maker by nature—sometimes I just make them so I can cross things off! I'm pretty certain it all began with Steve and those index cards he'd ask us to fill out. At first, mine were filled with all the big skills I wanted to learn. There were double backs off bars, difficult series on beam, and floor combinations that I could only imagine. Goal setting was really important to Steve, and he taught his gymnasts that it should be important to us, too.

Pretty soon I started to expand my goals to things like making it to States and doing better in a competition than I had done at my last meet. One of the first major goals I had was breaking an 8 on bars. I had that one for a long time, and I still remember the first time I broke the 8 barrier and got an 8.35. After that I scored in the 8's a lot, but the point wasn't so much the score as reaching my goal and then setting a higher one.

• goal setting as a way of life •

Goal setting has touched every aspect of my life—especially school. A's were always my goal, and I'd do whatever I had to get them. I'd study until 2:00 A.M., do tons of extra-credit work, stay after school, and meet with my teachers—whatever it took, I'd get those A's. That's the amazing thing about setting goals. You work hard until you can see them, eventually your fingertips brush them, and finally your hands grasp onto them like the high bar and you pull yourself up and over the goal. I love that feeling!

One of my biggest goals when I was younger was to try to be a good person, and to keep peace with my family. I was a middle child . . . the peacemaker. If my sister and brother were fighting, I'd try to settle things. Tessa and I didn't fight very much, but when we did I'd make up quickly so we could be best friends again.

• goals and gymnastics •

I think that to be a competitive athlete, you have to be goal-oriented. People always ask if one of my main gymnastics goals has been to win. That's never been the most important thing for me. If winning is your number-one priority and you fall short of that, then you're a loser. I don't think anyone can ever be a loser if they're competing—if they're out there doing something they enjoy.

My goal for every competition is the same as the one I had for my first one: to hit my routines and do what I practiced. It doesn't matter whether I'm competing in an invitational in Oklahoma or the Olympic Games, because in my mind they're both the same competition. They're the same four events, the same routines, and I don't think I should try harder at one meet than at the next. Consistency is key in gymnastics, and having the same goals helps me reach the level of excellence I'm always striving for.

Believe it or not, the Olympics was never even a goal for me. When I talk to young gymnasts, a lot of them tell me that they've wanted to be in the Olympics since they were born. But I never cared. I didn't even know what they were when I was a little kid. I never watched them on television—I still haven't seen much of them to this day. I saw a few of my routines from 1992 and a few highlights from 1996, but that's it!

These medals mean a lot to me. © *Garrison Photography—Edmond*

My early goals as a gymnast went from making States to becoming eligible for Regionals. After I made Regionals, my next goal was to try for Elite, the highest level of competitive gymnastics. After that it was Nationals; then my goal was to go to my first international competition. It was only in 1990, when the Olympics were two years away, that I started to even think about them becoming a goal. And then, of course, I thought it'd be amazing. But by that time I understood what it would take to get there.

I don't think when you're five years old you can know that the Olympics are what you want to do, because you don't know what it takes to get there, and you don't know what an honor it is to be able to compete in them. If you can't understand that, or if you can't feel that, then I don't think you're really ready to compete in the Olympics.

For me, things just kind of all flowed together. But the Olympics were never my main goal. If I hadn't made the U.S. team, it wouldn't have been the end of everything. It wouldn't have been like, "Oh, I wasted all those years trying to make the Olympic team and I didn't make it." I had fun all those years and accomplished so many of my goals that there was no way I could lose.

• school •

Not finishing school would have definitely made me feel like I'd lost something invaluable. School has always been one of my biggest goals. It's incredibly important to me. When I was finishing my junior year, Steve suggested I home-school instead of going to my local high school. It would only be for a year, he pointed out. Was it that big a deal if I didn't graduate from high school with my class?

"What if I don't make the Olympic team?" I asked myself. It was a possibility that I needed to think about as well as what was going to happen after the Olympics even if I did make the team. It's amazing to be able to represent your country and compete in the Games, but when they're over, they're over. And if you let important things in your life slide, it's hard to pick them up again. I'd always enjoyed going to a regular school and meeting people who weren't involved in gymnastics. It seemed a shame to miss out on graduating with Edmond North High School's class of 1995. So I decided to stay in school and graduate on time, and I also made the 1992 U.S. women's gymnastics team.

Whether to attend classes came up again before the 1996 Olympics. This time I was a student at the University of Oklahoma, and I decided to continue part-time so I could train yet still attend school. Of course, I was thrilled to make the 1996 team, but even if I hadn't, I knew that the Olympics weren't going to affect the rest of my life the way a college education would. Education is my future—it's how I'm going to get a job, help support my family, and find fulfillment later in life.

Me and Jaycie Phelps.

• friends •

It's always been pretty difficult for me to find the time to make new friends. That's been one of my goals this year—making friends at college so I have a better balance in my life. Most of my best friends are my teammates at Dynamo and my tour "family," but it's important to have other friends. Now I can work out with the girls on the University of Oklahoma gymnastics team part of the week and have time for a social life. I'm meeting a lot of new people—the students come from all over the country—and starting friendships.

Do I worry about making new friends—do I think they all want something from me? I guess I keep it in the back of my mind, and sometimes I can tell, but for the most part I think people mean well. I try to keep a positive attitude. Yeah, some people just want to meet me and hang out because I'm Shannon Miller, Olympic gymnast. But being a gymnast is what I do, that's what I've worked hard for, so if they want to meet me because of that, great. It just means that they're watching and that they enjoy what I do. It doesn't mean someone is a bad person or that they want something for the wrong reason.

I'm lucky, because I live in Oklahoma and everyone is so nice here. When I go to classes, no one treats me differently. No big deal. I'm not bombarded with questions by either the professors at the university or the students on campus. They treat me like a normal, regular person—which I am! It gives me hope that my goal of having friends outside of the gym is a realistic and attainable one.

• a nongoal: catching up •

This is one goal I don't need to worry about achieving. People think I must have missed out on many everyday things by being a gymnast. Yet I don't feel like I've missed out at all. I go to school, have friends, eat dinner with my family—everything "normal" people do. Then I add to it with being able to travel all over the world, do endorsements, make appearances, act, perform on the John Hancock Tour of World Gymnastics Champions, and do gymnastics clinics. I don't have to work nine to five or spend my entire day inside. My play time in the gym and traveling and meeting people are my job. You can't ask for a better profession than that!

• growing-up goals •

Things have changed a lot since the 1996 Olympics. Moving into my own place opened up a whole new world . . . of laundry to do, bills to pay, cleaning, and cooking! I never thought about those things before—they seemed to get done by "magic," although I'm sure my parents wouldn't agree. Of course they did my laundry and stocked our cabinets with my favorite foods because they love me . . . but now it's my responsibility to find time to accomplish those things. Sometimes I succeed and the bills are paid, my apartment is clean, the laundry is done, and my refrigerator is full. Other times I shove the dirty laundry in my closet and order take-out! I try to cut myself some slack and remember that goals have to be flexible and that attaining them requires dedication and constant work.

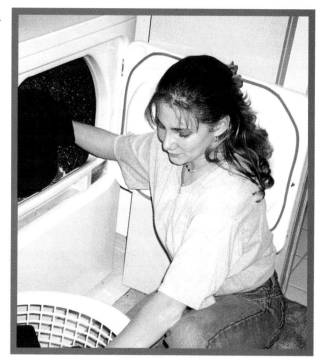

When I moved out of my parents' house, another one of my goals was to take over my business affairs. It was a real adjustment, because my parents handled the business end of my career so that I could train without being distracted. However, once I was in my twenties, it was important to me to take the pressure off my parents. My mom didn't need to be called at work every day to answer questions about me

Why is there always laundry to do?

Promoter Stan Feig, me, Sheryl Shade, Dominique Moceanu, and Bela Karolyi. *Courtesy of Shade Global*

or to set up appearances. She had her own job to do, and for as long as I can remember, my career was her second job. It was time for me to take control.

One of the first things I did was hire a new agent, Sheryl Shade. We work really well together, and I'm on the phone with her almost every day, going over my schedule of appearances and charity work and various other engagements. I think I'm handling the change pretty well.

In order to alter the format of my life so drastically, I made a new goal sheet:

The high-glam photo shoot for the book *Balancing Act.*

• goals for today •

1. Taking time for myself.
2. Being more efficient.
3. Letting go of the little things.
4. Trying to relax.
5. Realizing I can't do everything—
but that it's sure fun to try!

I've always been the kind of person who believes that if I want something done, it's better to do it myself. That way I know it's going to be done the way I want it. Just when I've taken charge of my life, I see that I have to let other people, like my agent, help me out. Once I had a taste of what it's like to be in control, it was tough putting decisions in someone else's hands. But just as finding the right coach was important, so was finding the right agent. I'm really happy with my choice, and finally I'm starting to ease up a bit.

Then there's the relaxation thing. My entire career has been unbelievably structured: this many hours for practice, that many hours to study, days before a meet, minutes before an event, seconds to make minuscule adjustments and stick landings. It used to be that when reporters asked me what my daily schedule was, I could tick off everything I did from the moment I woke up until the time I lay down at night.

All of a sudden I don't have a normal schedule. I don't know what I'm doing day to day, because at a moment's notice I might have to fly to New York for a photo shoot or to Los Angeles for a benefit. For someone who has lived her life knowing what's going to happen a week, a month, and a year from now, this new, unstructured lifestyle is very challenging.

Since the 1996 Olympics, I'm getting better at being more laid-back. When my bags didn't show up for the World University Games in Rome, I actually laughed. When I miss a cardio workout, I find time to go for a run or do my errands riding my bike. I try to be really efficient so that I have time for myself, to be a student, and to see a movie or at least e-mail friends.

It's hard to realize that I can't control everything anymore. But I guess that's part of life. I've lived a good portion of my twenty-one years in the gym—in a world where I had a lot of control. But life doesn't always let you tell it where to go. I've had to learn to let my lists slide a bit and just take things as they come, one day at a time.

• goals for the future •

After the Olympics, everyone started asking what my new goals were. The biggest question was: "Are you going to try to compete in the Olympic Games again?" My answer is a simple one: I don't know. The year 2000 is way too far ahead; I don't know what I'm going to be doing next January, let alone two years from now. What I can say is that I'm going to keep training, because I love gymnastics. I'm going to compete professionally and do the John Hancock Tour each year. And if something comes up internationally that sounds interesting, I'll train for it and compete.

Doing a promotional voice-over.

Right now, though, finishing college before I'm thirty is my main goal! I'm studying math and physics at the moment, but I'm not sure what I'll get my degree in. All I know is that I want to go to graduate school.

It's hard to say in this book exactly what I want to do with my life. I don't want to get stuck with any one thing. Right now I'm in the fortunate position of trying out many new things. In addition to pursuing my college degree, I'm doing some motivational speaking, appearances, and acting.

My first acting role wasn't too big a stretch—I played myself! I was in an episode of *Saved by the Bell*. I was nervous at first, but once they brought the audience in (just like in competition) I was fine. The show was a blast; I had so much fun, and the cast was really nice and supportive.

There are a few life goals that have never changed for me. One is getting married and having a family. Family has always been really important, and I'm looking forward to the time when I can have children—although I'm not in any rush! I've always wanted to design my own home, too. It will definitely be in the Midwest, but beyond that I don't know what kind of house, how big, or when it'll be built. I'm only twenty-one years old!

Here's a list of some of my future goals. Don't hold me to them, though. Right now I'm in a constant state of change!

• goals for tomorrow •

1. Keep training, touring, and competing.
2. Learn new gymnastics skills.
3. Stay in touch with friends from the 1996 Olympics and my most recent gymnastics tour, the John Hancock Tour.
4. Finish college.
5. Be open to trying new things.
6. Work more with my favorite charities, such as the Red Ribbon Celebration and the Children's Miracle Network.
7. Stay in close touch with my family and see them more often.
8. Go skiing again! I went skiing for the first time since I was five last December, and I loved it.

Ready to hit the slopes!

When we have a break from the tour, we shop till we drop!

9. Commentate on gymnastics, pursue motivational speaking, and keep acting.
10. Have fun!

Shannon's Advice: Setting goals for yourself can help you accomplish things in every aspect of your life. But goals have to be realistic and flexible. And even if they're not reached, it doesn't mean you're a loser. To me, true winners are people who go for what they want. And just the act of trying to improve yourself—the decision to broaden your horizons and reach a new level—makes you a winner.

Shannon's Golden Rule: Face each day with the expectation of achieving good, rather than the dread of falling short.

training

June 1992

Dear Diary,

I made the 1992 U.S. Olympic women's gymnastics team today! I'm so excited I can barely believe it—especially considering the fact that last month there was a chance I wouldn't be able to compete at the Olympic trials. I had an accident three months ago, and the doctors thought I might not be healed in time. And even if I was, there was a possibility that losing all that training time would really hurt my performance.

Looking back, it's still hard to believe how I got hurt. Right before the World Championships, I was doing a compulsory bar dismount and Steve pulled out the mat for my last routine (that's normal). Everything was going well, and then I just pulled in, hit my feet on the bar, and came down on the ground with my arms first.

I've fallen off the bars a million times, but even before the pain came, something told me that this was different. I just lay on the floor for a few moments. I didn't cry or move or anything. It was like my brain and my body were trying to assess whether or not I'd hurt myself, and how bad it was.

"Steve," I called. "Steve?" He came running over and told me to stay still. Anytime his gymnasts fall, he wants us to freeze until he's done a body check and made sure we're okay. Usually we're fine, and we get back up and try again whatever we messed up. But this time he told me that I'd have to stay down.

I looked over at my left elbow and saw that it was bent the wrong way—totally dislocated. Quickly I turned away and Steve covered my arm with a sweatshirt because he didn't want me to see it. He had one of the other girls take off my grip (the hand covering that prevents skin tears), and I just kept waiting for him to pick up my left arm and pop the elbow back in the joint. It's going to be okay, *I told myself.* He'll just pop it back in and with twenty minutes of ice I'll be ready to go to beam.

But Steve didn't pop it back in. Instead, he called my parents and drove me to the hospital. I swear, it was the bumpiest road in the world. My elbow throbbed with pain. As we drove, it started to sink in that my injury was more serious than I'd thought.

Steve said he didn't want to try to fix my elbow because he wasn't sure if there might be a bone chip. If there was, he could do more damage. He wanted the doctors to look at it and get X rays taken.

The X rays seemed to take forever. I just kept wondering, Why don't they pop it back in and get this over with? *I just assumed that as soon as they did, it would stop hurting and aching. Finally they did put it back into place, but things weren't over.*

My doctor met with Steve, my parents, and me—he let Steve explain what was wrong, since he knew I'd feel more at ease hearing the news from him.

"Here's the thing," Steve told me. "There's still a bone chip floating around in there. The doctors can put you in a cast for six weeks and it'll heal up and reattach by itself." We both knew there was only a month and a half before the Olympic trials. My first Olympic trials.

"There's another option," Steve said. "They can put in a screw and reattach the bone chip. They're saying it'll be healed in six weeks." Six weeks? *I thought worriedly.* How am I going to stay fit? How am I going to make the Olympic team with only two weeks to train before trials?

My parents and I talked it over and decided that surgery was my best option. I went into the operating room that night and spent the next day resting at home. I never took pain pills—it just didn't hurt enough to convince me they were necessary. The doctors had put my arm in a splint, which they said I had to wear for five days,

44

and had wrapped my arm. I returned to the gym one day later! Steve devised a way that I could train even with the splint. He had me do a lot of conditioning and running. I did double backs on the trampoline, vaulted with one arm, and did one-handed back handsprings. I was surprised at how much I could do!

Steve told me that the main thing was to keep my air sense and body movements, and make sure the rest of my body stayed in shape. That way, when my arm healed I'd be ready to go. Each day at the end of practice, Steve and I worked on keeping the flexibility in my left arm. We'd straighten it out a little more each day and make sure that the scar tissue didn't cause it to lock. That part hurt, but it was worth it because I'm going to my first Olympics in Barcelona, Spain! I only hope I can make everyone proud.

• achieving your dreams— time, training, and tenacity •

Practicing with Steve at Dynamo. © *Dave Black 1998*

So what does it take to train to be a gymnast? You have to love the sport. You need a great coach, supportive parents, and the ability to motivate yourself. And a little natural ability doesn't hurt. If you want to take it up a step and aim to become a competitive gymnast, you have to be mentally strong and prepared to take on the workload of going to the gym every day, rain or shine. But most of all, you have to accept the fact that it takes a ton of hard work.

• no one starts off on top— it's a step-by-step process •

The learning process for developing big skills in gymnastics is a long one. I remember the first time I learned a double layout on the floor. Steve had me start on a tumble track (a long, narrow trampoline with a thick pile of mats at the end). We began with high layouts. When he felt confident that I was ready, he told me to go for the double. On any new skill, Steve spots me until he thinks I'm going to be safe trying the skill by myself. I always know that if Steve says I can do it, I can. I may not make the skill, but I'm going to be safe and land somewhere around my feet or my butt, not on my head.

It's still nerve-racking trying a new skill—even if your coach has all the confidence in the world in you. But it's more exciting, more of an adrenaline rush, than scary. Usually the first attempt goes the best, because you've got all that energy as you run down the tumble track. I'm always more relaxed on my second try, and that means I end up landing low. In fact, sometimes Steve calls out, "I want to see fear like in the first one," so that I remember the feeling and put more into my second try.

I really enjoy training for new skills—especially on the beam. Usually you start off practicing the skills on the floor. Once you've got them, you draw a line on the floor and practice making them on the line. When you've got that mastered, you go to the low beam. I have to admit that I rarely practice new skills on the low beam. For some reason I can't make a series of skills (like back handspring, back handspring, back somersault) on a low beam to save my life! I go straight from the floor to the high beam. And usually I haven't quite gotten the series down before I get to the high beam, because I don't work series of skills well on the floor, either! Call me crazy!

Most girls pile mats right beneath the beam so that if they fall off while trying a new skill, they don't actually fall anywhere. For a big skill, I usually put mats about halfway up to the beam because it's more comfortable for me to learn when I know that falling off really *means* falling off. That's the interesting and challenging thing about gymnastics—every gymnast is different. And it's figuring out the best way you need to train, and finding someone who can work with you and understand what makes you tick, that lead to more fun, improvement, and success, at whatever level you're aiming for.

• the coach-gymnast bond •

I'm fortunate to have found a coach right at the start of my career whom I clicked with. A lot of girls move around from gym to gym. My good friend Kim Zmeskal stayed with Bela Karolyi until he retired—now she's with another top-level coach, Mary Lee Tracy. Most gymnasts are constantly trying out new coaches to find someone who's right for them.

I can't tell you how important it is to be able to communicate with your coach and vice versa. Imagine that you're out there on the floor getting ready for a second vault, and your coach is way down at the other end. You don't have time to run over and discuss your vault, but if you're in tune with each other, a small hand movement or look can tell you exactly what you need to know. Maybe it's just to make a tiny correction, like keeping your arms in, or maybe it's reminding you to stick your landing. Either way, that hand movement or look gives you the confidence you need.

Sometimes I think the reason Steve and I work so well together is that I started with him at such a young age. He taught me the right way to do things from the beginning, and I grew up looking at situations the same way he does. The bottom line, though, is that we want the same thing. When you

Steve coaching me at Olympic Fest 1989 . . . we've been together a long time. © *Dave Black 1998*

and your coach have the same goals, it's a lot easier to work together. I know that when he is yelling at me, he only wants the best for me, just like he knows when to push and when to leave me alone.

My most difficult moments were after the 1992 Olympics. I was in the middle of my rebellious teenage years and I started challenging Steve whenever I was afraid of learning a new skill. One day he told me to go for a move and I wouldn't do it. It wasn't that I didn't trust him, it was that I started thinking about the consequences of my actions. I started crying out of frustration, and arguing that I wasn't ready. Steve told me to leave practice. He knew he wasn't going to get any more work out of me that day. So I grabbed my bag and stormed out of the gym.

Usually gymnasts who've been sent home wait in the lobby for their mom or dad to pick them up. It's a horrible feeling. Everyone else is out there practicing and you're in the lobby wasting time. I *hate* wasting time. Plus, when your parents arrive you have to explain why you're not out on the floor practicing.

Anyway, Steve kicked me out. But instead of waiting in the lobby, I headed out to the parking lot. I was sixteen and I'd just gotten my driver's license. Steve had forgotten that. So when he came looking for me in the lobby to talk about what'd happened, he didn't understand why I wasn't there. One of the other gymnasts told him I had my license, and I think it hit him then that I wasn't a little girl anymore, and he'd have to remember that when he was coaching me.

Mom and Dad were furious when I got home. I was a new driver and I'd driven on the highway in rush-hour traffic. And I was upset that I hadn't had the discipline to throw a move that Steve knew was safe for me.

It took a little while for me to remember what was important—that I wanted to shoot for the World Championships and maybe another chance to be in the Olympics. Once I did, my bad attitude disappeared and I buckled down again.

• the long haul •

While a great coach is vital, the ability to see the big picture and commit to the long haul of day-in, day-out hard work is equally important in training. Sometimes it's tough. There are aches and pains. You get rips in your hands, your muscles are sore from conditioning, and sometimes you pull muscles and that hurts. But I have very little memory of the pain because that's not what stands out for me. The toughest thing about any injury is the fact that I want to be out there, doing skills, practicing, and competing, and my body won't let me.

• what goes into elite-level gymnastics training? •

Before the 1992 Olympics I would practice five or six hours a day, six days each week. The rest of Steve's gymnasts at Dynamo Gymnastics maintained normal schedules. Before the 1996 Games, I trained six to eight hours a day, six days a week, along with several other girls at the Elite level, including Jennie Thompson, who was training for trials. In both cases, we'd start with fifteen minutes of running to loosen up our bodies. The next forty-five minutes were for conditioning: sit-ups, pull-ups, squats, things like that.

After the first hour, Steve would have us work three events in a day of practice. We usually traded off vault and floor because they're both big leg events. Beam and bars are more important to do every day since they involve a high degree of precision and balance. It takes about an hour to an hour and a half for

Steve and I share silly times, too.

the whole group of gymnasts (depending on size and on the event) to get through both their compulsory and optional routines on an event.

Of course, I didn't train for six or eight hours straight! Usually it was four in the morning and four in the evening. I've seen some made-for-television movies that depict young gymnasts dragging themselves to practice before the sun rises. We never worked out in the early, early morning. Your body just doesn't function then!

• training, eating, drinking, and sleeping on competition day •

Once it's time for a major competition, the training schedule changes. We slowly taper down, and on the day of a meet we just have a really light workout—more touching the equipment than actually doing routines. Then we return to our hotel, and I usually take a nap, watch TV, or read.

I *always* eat lunch before a meet. Not a lot, but a good meal. I like grilled chicken and vegetables or a chicken sandwich and fruit—something with substance—because it's usually six or seven hours before the competition ends. They can run really long, especially by the time you take the mandatory drug test and meet with the media. So it's really important to eat, because it can be many hours before you get your next meal and you're going to need energy.

I try to drink a lot of water before, during, and after a competition. At least that's what I do now. I never used to, and it caught up with me. Two weeks after the 1996 Olympics I was hospitalized with severe stomach cramps. It turned

52

Posing with five of the Magnificent Seven for a *People* cover shoot. Boy, was it hot!

out that I was totally dehydrated. It happened not during the competition, but afterward—during what I referred to as Hell Week.

Hell Week is the week after the Olympics. That's when agents, parents, and anyone even remotely involved with the team fights over who's doing what and when, and what the team's commitments should be. During that time, I was trying to figure out my own life, in between making appearances my agent was lining up for me.

I was so busy that I never thought about drinking enough water. I'd just have some fruit and whatever food I could grab on my way to wherever I was going at the moment. The result was that I got horrible stomach cramps and couldn't even move. My parents took me to the hospital and the doctors pumped in about a gallon of fluids. I gained five pounds in twenty-four hours, and it was a rotten experience. I was puffy and bloated for days. Since then, I carry a big bottle of water with me everywhere I go.

After I eat, I get ready for the competition. I fix my hair, put on my leotard, and apply my makeup. I don't know why I bother with the makeup, though. In competition it usually sweats off after the first warm-up event.

My favorite meets to prepare for are the international ones . . . because you have to leave the hotel earlier than usual. (You'll see why that's important a little later.) Traffic is always an unknown factor, and missing a meet because the driver miscalculated how long it would take to get to the arena would be terrible. On the way to the meet, I usually sleep. In fact, it's a running joke with all the other gymnasts that I can sleep anywhere, anytime. If it's a forty-five-minute ride, I sleep the entire way. When I wake up, I'm relaxed and refreshed. It's like my body just shuts down for a while, and within five minutes of getting up I'm ready to go! I'm a firm believer in taking care of myself. I couldn't be an Elite gymnast if I wasn't.

Once I get to the arena, I usu-

All that training paid off at Worlds. © *Dave Black 1998*

ally lie on the mat by myself and mentally go over my routines (we're early, so there's time). I see myself doing each one perfectly. I know some athletes practice both the right and wrong way in their head, but I believe you should only have what's right in your mind. So I envision the correct way to do each routine. When it's time for the meet, I'm as relaxed as I can be, rested, and mentally prepared to compete.

• not training versus training •

Here's a good example of how *not* training can be just as important as training! A few weeks before the 1994 World Championships, to be held April 19 to 24 in Brisbane, Australia, I pulled a stomach muscle. It left me unable to do even the simplest skills. Any kid who has ever tried to do a kip on the uneven bars (a swing on the low bar where your legs are parallel with the floor and you pull up onto the bar) knows that there's just no way you can do it without a strong stomach. I couldn't do a kip, let alone pull in my legs, hold my feet up, do a layout on the beam, or get through any of my big skills on the floor.

Steve decided I should try to make the World Championships team anyway. That involved competing in Nationals, where I only needed to place in the top five on one event to make the team since I'd been on the 1992 Olympic team. I went to Nationals and barely muddled through my one vault. I placed in the top five and earned a spot on the World Championship Team, but we still weren't sure I'd be able to compete in Brisbane.

Usually right before a meet, training time tapers down. But I hadn't been able to completely practice any of my routines the week before Nationals—just bits and pieces that didn't hurt my stomach. I spent the final days before the meet in constant training. As my stomach muscle healed we kept stepping up my work-outs. In the end, things really came together. I won both the gold on the beam and my second all-around gold medal at Worlds, becoming the only American ever to win in two consecutive years. But the thing that helped me to win wasn't training—it was knowing when *not* to train.

• training changes over time•

My training schedule has changed a lot since the 1996 Olympics. Now it's pretty sporadic. Steve lets me go into the gym anytime I want, whether anyone is there or not. Sometimes I'll go in the morning, when no coaches or gymnasts are around. I'll work out for about three hours, but I won't do any release moves on the bars where I need a spot, or any skills on the vault, beam, and floor that aren't safe.

I try to get to the gym four days a week. Sometimes my schedule just doesn't allow it, and I have to work out in other cities and gyms. No matter what, I try to get some cardiovascular exercise each day. I really like aerobics, and when that's not available I force myself to run (it's just so boring!). If Steve and I de-cide that I'm going to a big competition, I step up my training to get ready for it. The thing is, I just don't need as much training as I used to in order to get ready for a meet. I can work two to three hours a day for four days a week and keep all of my skills. For me, it's mostly about staying flexible and keeping my strength.

• here's what i do to stay in shape •

1. Aerobics
2. Running
3. Biking
4. Walking
5. Swimming
6. Hiking
7. Gymnastics (of course)
8. In-line skating
9. Step class
10. Weight lifting

Shannon's Advice: No matter what, be active. Do activities you love and enjoy. I've spent so much time in a gym that I just like being outside. Whether it's running, in-line skating, hiking, or biking, it's important to have fresh air and exercise.

Shannon's Golden Rule: Your mind produces all action. Stay healthy and focused in mind and body!

I like in-line skating so much that I thought I'd try ice skating . . . it's so much fun!

57

stress

August 1992

Dear Diary,

I just returned from my first Olympics! The Games were held in Barcelona, Spain. They were everything I could have imagined, and more. I've been surprised over how many people have asked me if the gymnasts were stressed out. People have commented that we didn't act like a team and that we didn't support each other. First of all, I can't speak for anyone else, but gymnastics doesn't stress me out. I love it and that's why I do it. If I weren't enjoying myself, I'd have quit a long time ago. Maybe the confusion started because people don't necessarily understand the way a gymnastics meet works—especially when it's the Olympics.

It's not that the U.S. gymnasts weren't supporting each other. The fact is, we're not always out on the competition floor at the same time. There are different sessions—morning and evening. I have evening session, which means I work out in the morning, return to my room, rest and eat, then return to the arena for evening competition. Sometimes when a teammate is competing, you're in a separate gym, warming up and preparing for your next event. It's not that we don't want to cheer for each other—it depends on who has what session.

And even if I am in the arena, usually I don't have time to watch my friends compete because I have to focus on my own routine, mentally rehearse, and make sure I don't miss the call to compete. Can you imagine cheering for someone and missing an event? No one on the team takes it personally. We understand that we're all trying to accomplish the same thing—hitting our routines. And we know that our teammates are rooting for us, even if they're not voicing it right then.

Each gymnast has to focus on what she's doing. I don't watch other athletes compete because no matter what they do—whether it's a perfect routine or a big mistake—it doesn't affect me or my performance. I can't change what happens to other gymnasts. All I can control is what I do, and my goal is to do my very best for myself and my team.

You know what kind of hurts me? When I hear people say that we're so stoic, that we have no personality. That we're just robots. Maybe it's because we're younger than many competitive athletes. I don't ever hear commentators saying that Jackie Joyner-Kersee or Michael Jordan should be joking around during a race or a game. No one asks where their smiles are. They're concentrating on the task at hand, just like gymnasts do at a meet. I joke a lot at the gym, but when a competition rolls around I get serious. And considering the safety concerns of the sport, being stoic and focused is downright necessary. It's the serious side that the general public sees, because the cameras aren't rolling during practices and everyday life.

• the stress test •

Everyone has stress in their life. Whether it's an algebra test, a new job, your first date, or getting along with friends, no one can pass the stress test with flying colors. But it's how you handle stress that leads to winning or losing situations.

I remember lying on my bed in the Olympic Village in Barcelona, Spain, on the night before my first event in 1992. "Please, God," I whispered, "help me get through this." At that moment I could have let my fears, stress, and worries overwhelm me. Instead, I told myself that I had done the same routines I'd do the next day thousands of times. I'd trained for the Olympics, and I knew I could hit my routines and stick my landings. It was my first Olympics, I reminded myself. Whatever I did, I'd already won because I'd made the team and I was representing the United States at the Olympics.

No one expected much from me at the 1992 Olympic Games. I felt pretty lucky to be the underdog, because there was no pressure. The focus was on Kim Zmeskal, not Shannon Miller, and that was fine with me. I know now from my experiences at the 1996 Olympics that it must have been really hard on Kim.

The 1992 U.S. women's Olympic gymnastics team: Betty Okino, Wendy Bruce, Dominique Dawes, me, Kerri Strug, and Kim Zmeskal. © *Dave Black 1998*

She had to do many interviews, and a lot of media attention was directed toward her. There was no way it couldn't have taken away from her focus on the competition. It also put her under a lot more pressure because people were expecting so much from her.

But in 1992 I didn't know about any of that. All I knew was that I was the underdog and that I loved that position. The 1992 Olympics were a lot of fun. I won silvers for the beam and all-around and three bronze medals. I loved the experience.

• roll with it •

Sometimes the best way to handle stress is to roll with it. Remember my journal entry about the trip to Rome and how I had to do some crazy flying to get to the World University Games? Well, crazy is an understatement. And if I hadn't been able to let go of the stress, I wouldn't have ended up winning the all-around. The truth is, I would've been so frazzled that I probably wouldn't have even placed.

Here's what was *supposed* to happen: I was supposed to go from a training camp in Chicago to an award ceremony in Denver, then to Hartford, Connecticut, for a one-day clinic at a gymnastics camp. From Connecticut I was supposed to be driven to Kennedy Airport in New York and then board a flight to Rome for the World University Games.

Here's what *really* happened: I was in Chicago for three days, no problem. When I got on the plane to Denver, a flight attendant came up to me and asked if I was Shannon Miller. I said yes, thinking he recognized me and might want an autograph. Instead, he handed me tickets to Italy with my name on them. I knew I hadn't dropped them, because I hadn't had them—I was supposed to pick the tickets up in Denver. Much later, I learned that Steve had had them delivered to the airport in Chicago after discovering that he accidentally had them. I should have known then that the next few days were not going to be smooth sailing.

I flew to Denver and was there for two days. I trained and went to an award ceremony honoring the Magnificent Seven (the 1996 U.S. women's Olympic gymnastics team), which gave me the chance to catch up with my Olympic teammates. After that dinner, I had a flight to Hartford that left the Denver airport a little after midnight. Since I had a few hours to kill, I went back to the hotel to pack.

The driver who was supposed to take me to the airport had told me earlier that if he picked me up at 11:15 P.M., we'd have more than enough time to get to the airport, since the drive only took twenty or thirty minutes. When 11:15 rolled around, the driver hadn't called up to my room. At 11:30 I started to get antsy, so I called down to the front desk to get a cab. The concierge said I didn't need one because my driver was waiting in the lobby. I called a bellman because I had a ton of luggage (I was going to be traveling for a month) and we raced down to the lobby, where the driver had been waiting all along. I didn't bother to ask why he hadn't called, because we were so late that nothing mattered but catching my flight.

As usual, I fell asleep on the way to the airport. When we arrived, I realized that the drive had taken forty-five minutes—not twenty or thirty. I missed my flight, and it was nearly 1:00 A.M., so there were no more flights going out. I started to get stressed, but there was a 5:45 A.M. flight leaving that morning (only a few hours away). I had the driver take me back to the hotel so that I could sleep for a couple of hours. I figured I'd still make it to the clinic on time, I'd just be a little tired from traveling.

I made the 5:45 A.M. flight and flew out of Denver to Cincinnati, where I was supposed to change planes. But we had a rain delay, so by the time we landed I'd missed my flight to Hartford. I called my agent so that she could call the gym owner and tell him I was going to be a little late. Then I went to a ticket agent and he rerouted me through Newark, New Jersey, so I could still get to Hartford that day. I had to run to make the flight and I was the last person on. As the doors closed, I was 100 percent sure that my bags hadn't been loaded onto the plane. What if they got lost and never made it to Italy for my competition?

When we arrived at Newark I ran to make my flight to Hartford. "I'm sorry, you don't have a reservation," the ticket agent told me. The last agent had forgotten to make reservations for me when my flight was switched from Delta to Continental. The Continental agent was really nice and he put me at the top of the list for standby. However, the flight before mine had been canceled and this next one was overbooked by fifty. I got on the phone and called my agent so that she could tell the gym owner that I was going to be really, really late.

By the time the plane got me there, I was extremely late. I had an hour-long drive to the gymnastics camp, which would give me only about ten minutes to sign autographs—not nearly enough time. As much as I didn't want to disappoint any of the fans who would show up at the camp, participating for ten minutes just didn't make sense. I called my agent and together we regretfully decided that not only would it have been an extremely short appearance, but making it put my flight to Italy in jeopardy.

I was able to catch a flight from Hartford to Kennedy Airport, which was about an hour away. I still had no luggage, but all I was focused on was making my plane. The competition was only one day away, and if I didn't get there on time, I'd be letting down the team. When the plane arrived at Kennedy, I sprinted to the international terminal and just made it in time to get on the flight to Rome. Unfortunately, my bags didn't make the flight with me. They

The fans have always supported me. *Photo by Gene Stafford*

were somewhere between Denver, Cincinnati, Newark, Hartford, and Kennedy airports.

So what's the message of that story? Just that my head could have literally exploded if I'd let the stress of that week get to me. At a certain point—I think it was on the runway in ninety-five-degree heat—I just had to shrug and roll with the situation. I had no control over the plane or the flight schedules. So instead of worrying and stressing, I did the best I could and tried to laugh at the craziness of it all.

• olympic stress •

Sometimes it's impossible not to let the pressure of a situation get to you. Yet it wasn't the gymnastics that stressed me out in Atlanta. It was the fact that people in my country were going to see everything firsthand. On the one side, that was amazing for all the U.S. athletes. I can't even describe how it felt to enter the arena and hear "USA" being chanted by thousands. The level of support was overwhelming.

On the other side, I had a lot more obligations because the Games were in the United States. I finally understood how much pressure Kim Zmeskal had been under in 1992, and how interviews and media appointments could really hurt a gymnast's focus. I tried not to do any interviews beginning a month before the Games, but it was impossible not to have some contact with the press.

This time, as I lay in my bed the night before the Games began, I really felt the pressure. I wasn't the underdog anymore. I just wanted to do well and not let my coaches or parents down. They had all been so supportive and put in the time and effort right along with me. I didn't want to let the United States down, either—the home crowd that cheered for and believed in me.

Whatever is going to happen is going to happen, I finally told myself. I'd trained hard for the Games. I'd overcome injuries and worked through them, and I knew I was as prepared as I was going to be. I also knew these Games might or might not be my last Olympics, and I just had to go into that arena and have fun. My teammates were a fantastic group of girls, and I wanted to enjoy competing with them. Most of all, I tried to remember why I had started gymnastics, what I loved about it, how fun it was being in front of a crowd, and that placements and winning didn't matter as much as doing my best out there.

It was hard to put things into perspective—especially before a competition as big as the Olympics. Steve's training really helped me at that moment, because he believes that the most important thing is to shoot for the top and only focus on what really matters. He'd always taught me never to look at scores or to watch other athletes compete. To this day, I don't begin a routine knowing that I need a 9.6 to win. Each time I shoot for that perfect score of 10.

Listening to Steve at the 1996 Olympics. *Photo by Gene Stafford*

The same holds when I take a final exam in school. I don't go into it knowing I need a 92 in order to get an A for the term. I go in aiming for a 100 each time. Usually I end up getting a higher grade than I need for an A, because I'm reaching for the top. The night before the 1996 Games began, I shifted my focus from letting people down and the pressure I felt to aiming for the best competition I'd ever had.

• the tears •

The 1996 Olympics were an unbelievable experience. The U.S. women's gymnastics team won a gold in the team competition, and I won a gold in the individual beam competition. Sometimes, though, the attention didn't focus on the glory of the Games, but rather on the tears of some of its youngest competitors, and the idea that maybe gymnasts aren't ready for the tension and stress of intense competition.

This is my chance to set the record straight about the tears millions of people watched fall during the Games. I don't cry when I'm stressed. Sometimes I do for injuries—but that's just because I want to be out on the floor performing. For me, frustration is the thing that gets the tears rolling. Some people yell, stamp on the floor, or break dishes. I cry. When I didn't perform as well as I knew I could during the 1996 Games, I cried out of frustration, because I knew I could have done better.

Gymnasts have upsets just like any other athletes. And cameras do capture our mistakes, and often the tears that follow. But shedding some tears doesn't mean gymnasts are unstable, or that we can't handle the stress or pressure of competition. At the Elite level, we train hard and expect results, and sometimes we're frustrated and disappointed by our attempts. When that happens, some of us cry as a way to deal with our emotions. I always feel better after a good cry, don't you?

• the top four things that could be stressful—if i let them •

1. The 2000 Olympics

People ask me if I'm going to be in the 2000 Olympics. I just finished the 1996 Olympics two years ago . . . the Sydney Games are too far away for me to think about. I don't know what I'm doing next week!

2. Are you going to coach?

I am not "just" a gymnast. Not that being a gymnast isn't a great thing, but I can do other things. Everyone seems to think that I'm either going to retire, keep training, coach, open my own gym, or become a judge. I guess I don't like being viewed so narrowly.

3. A messy apartment

It really bugs me when I can't keep my apartment clean. I love things clean, but there are days when all I have time for is coming home, doing a load of laundry, repacking, and leaving again. Sometimes I just drop my bag, throw everything out on the floor, toss a few things back in that I need that day for a trip, and leave. Needless to say, when I come back no magic genie has cleaned up and the place is a mess. I wish I had more time to clean, because I actually enjoy it!

4. What are you going to do with the rest of your life?

I'm only twenty-one years old! That's the time when most young adults are testing a zillion different options. I have the rest of my life ahead of me, and right now I'm not ready to be held to any one thing. I'm planning on having a career outside of gymnastics (that's why school has always been so important). I want the chance to excel at a lot of different things. While twenty-one is considered old in gymnastics, I feel like I've only begun the second chapter of my life.

• alleviating stress •

My time in the gym is a great way to alleviate stress. At the gym I don't have to think about anything but working out. It's the same with school. When I'm studying or in class, the last thing I think about is gymnastics. The two are entirely separate and they balance each other out really well.

The bottom line is that in gymnastics, just like anything else, you have to know what works for you and when a situation is too much to handle. There are so many levels of any sport or activity that everyone should be able to find something that fits into their life. For example, if you're interested in gymnastics but don't want to devote a lot of time to it, there are recreational clubs and tumbling classes. Troy, my brother, took gymnastics for a little bit, and he learned the strength, coordination, and flexibility that he needed for tae kwon do. Right now he's testing for his black belt!

As far as Elite gymnastics goes, you have to know what you can deal with. Not every girl is going to have the level of maturity needed to compete. And it's not just about competition. You've got to enjoy traveling and be able to handle all the details that go with visiting new places—like whether or not you can drink the water, what foods to avoid overseas (eating raw fish in certain places can lead to some pretty serious stomach bugs), plane flights, time changes, different currencies, and the difficulty of being away from home and family for weeks at a time.

For most gymnasts it's pretty obvious right from the start whether they enjoy competing or if it's too much for them. If they don't like it, it's not fun. And if it's not fun, they usually quit. It's rare to find a gymnast at the Elite level who lacks the maturity to handle the pressure of competition.

• the good guys •

Initially, for me, the most stressful part of gymnastics was dealing with the media. When I was younger, I wasn't very talkative with strangers. After the 1992 Games, I was thrown into a room with tons of reporters speaking different languages, with cameras, lights, and microphones. It was a frightening situation for a shy kid, but over time I learned how to handle interviews and it got a lot easier.

I recognize that the media are made up of real people, and most of them are good. I actually don't mind being interviewed, or the photographers and cameras. Basically, I've grown up with lenses five inches away from my face for most of my life—whether I'm crying, excited, or happy. I even like a lot of the cameramen. One in particular—a man named Kenny Woo—is a favorite. At the 1992 Olympics he went around the Barcelona arena dropping pennies. Kenny knew that some of the girls on the U.S. team believed that if they found a penny, it was good luck.

There's a photographer named Dave Black that I also really like. (Several of his pictures are in this book.) After the U.S. women's gymnastics team won the team gold in Atlanta, he was in tears. He'd watched us since we were nine or ten years old. As he took the Magnificent Seven's photo, Dave told us that our winning was the best thing he'd ever seen. Hearing that really touched me.

As the 1996 U.S. women's gymnastics team posed for that picture, I think we all felt the same way. Not all of us received individual medals. But each one of the Magnificent Seven—Amanda Borden, Amy Chow, Dominique Dawes, Dominique Moceanu, Jaycie Phelps, Kerri Strug, and myself—was happy, excited,

The 1996 U.S. women's Olympic gymnastics team: Amanda Borden, Dominique Dawes, Amy Chow, Jaycie Phelps, Dominique Moceanu, Kerri Strug, and me. © *Dave Black 1998*

and proud about her part in the team's accomplishment and for her teammates' individual successes. Whatever stress and pressure surrounded us was gone for that moment, and we hugged and enjoyed being friends—and gold medalists.

• the top ten ways i handle stress •

1. Sleep (not the most productive choice).
2. Be thankful that I'm so busy and have so many opportunities.
3. Watch television (especially *Seinfeld*).
4. Make a schedule of everything that needs to be done.
5. Fix the problem (if it's my messy apartment, I'll stay up until three in the morning to get it clean).
6. Exercise (it relaxes me so I can deal with the stress).
7. Listen to music.
8. Talk to family.
9. Call friends for a fun conversation.
10. Read and answer e-mail.

Shannon's Advice: Stress can't exist unless you let it. If something is bothering you, figure out why and then work to solve the problem. Sometimes I try to avoid a problem, but it just gets bigger and harder to deal with. Eventually, whatever is stressing you out will have to be faced. Do it sooner rather than later.

Shannon's Golden Rule: If you put your trust in God, He will adjust everything correctly.

the thrill of competition

September 1996

Dear Diary,

    I think it all started with Grandma. She's the one who taught me how to play all those board games. I'd play with her for hours until I beat her (lucky for me that grandmas never get tired of playing with their grandchildren). Monopoly was one of my favorites. Most people hate it because it takes forever, but I could sit with my family and play and play until I had the most money. And then there's checkers, which I love because there's a strategy to it. And Uno—I'm the queen of Uno!

    I figure it's Grandma's fault that I'm such a competitive person. Funny, in gymnastics and school I'm mostly competitive with myself, but deal out the cards, open up the Pictionary board, or set the timer for Scattergories and I play to win. Last night is a prime example.

    First, I have to say that I thought my competitive drive had decreased since the 1996 Olympics. I've been kind of tapering off at practice, focusing on schoolwork, and relaxing a bit. But then an old teammate of mine, Marianna Webster, came to town.

    It's not what you think. We didn't go to the gym or anything. We went to the mall and out to dinner. Afterward, we ran into a friend and decided to go to a movie. It was a clear, nice night and we were laughing and joking around as we walked to our cars in the parking lot. Marianna and I hopped in my car and my friend got in his. As we started to pull out of the lot, our eyes locked together, and an unspoken chal-

lenge passed between us: Who could get to the theater first? I love finding shortcuts—and saving time! I wasn't going to break any traffic laws, of course—I would never condone racing—but I knew all the turns to make and side roads to take. We'd definitely get there before he would. As my sports car sped through the Oklahoma night, I realized just how competitive I still am. After years of gymnastic meets, World Championships, and Olympics, I still want to win . . . no matter what the situation is!

Marianna suggested we stop for munchies rather than buy them at the movie theater, and it took every ounce of willpower to apply the brake and hang a left toward the grocery store. I would've won, I told her as we pulled into the store parking lot.

"A movie without munchies just isn't a movie," Marianna reminded me.

"You're right," I agreed. But I would've won.

• a competitive bone •

I don't believe that there's anyone in the world without a competitive bone in their body. Maybe it's as simple as getting the seat you want on the bus, or being the first in line to buy tickets to a concert. Perhaps it's being the best violinist in the school band or skiing a run down the mountain better than you've ever done it before.

Sometimes people just have the need to be first, last, best, smartest, or most talented. You might be competing against others, or just against yourself. Sometimes that drive is positive, and sometimes it works against you. But either way, the drive to compete pushes you forward, makes you try harder, and can end up helping you grow into a better, stronger person.

• competition and me •

For me, the competitive urge is almost always internal. Gymnastics is the best example. At a competition, I've never looked at other girls and thought, *That's the one I've got to beat.* It's always been me against me, or me against the equipment. Whether it's in practice or at a meet, I'm always trying to do the very best that I can. I love to win, I'm not going to say I don't, but in gymnastics winning isn't everything for me. It's how I feel about my performance that really matters.

The same holds true for school. I'm not competitive with other people—just with myself. Sure, I could take easy courses and coast through college, or try to get out of the work. But what would be the point? I'd just be wasting time and money. So I take harder courses and challenge myself to get A's. And *aiming* for A's has resulted in *earning* A's.

Practicing my floor routine in Atlanta. *Photo by Gene Stafford*

• that thrill •

I focus on my own performance in gymnastics, but there's nothing like the thrill of competition to pump me up and get me going. No matter how I'm feeling in practice, the moment I step into an arena I forget about my aching back, or the landings off the uneven bars that I couldn't seem to stick the week before, or that it's my fifth routine of the day. All I think about is that it's great to be out there doing something I love.

When I walk into a full arena, it's like everything changes in a split second. All of a sudden the atmosphere is electric. There are screaming fans, people yelling out, "It's Miller time," and chanting, "USA." My adrenaline starts

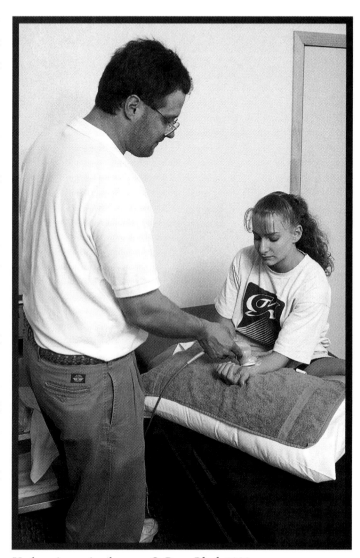

Undergoing wrist therapy. © *Dave Black 1998*

coursing and there's this burst of energy that makes me feel like I can do anything! It doesn't matter if a minute earlier I was feeling bad—the only thing that matters is what I do when I step onto the floor for my first event.

Right before the start of the 1996 Olympics I was having trouble with my wrist. I couldn't even get through a bar routine because holding on for the duration of my routine was impossible. I hadn't been able to train hard for the event, and I didn't have the strength or endurance I needed. Still, I knew from experience that when I stepped up to the bars adrenaline and the crowd's enthusiasm would get me through. And they did.

• a wave of noise •

I've always been taught not to listen to the crowd or the other things going on around me. I hear other gymnasts' music when I'm waiting to begin a routine, but once I start, I don't hear it at all. In fact, I couldn't tell you any of the music that was playing in any meet I've ever competed in.

Sometimes I hear the crowd oohing or gasping, but I don't think about whether or not it's for me. Another gymnast could have fallen off the beam while I'm doing my floor routine, or maybe someone slipped off the vault. I just tune out the sound and keep going.

It's not the same thing when the crowd applauds. I still don't pay attention to specifics, but I hear it like a wave of noise. It doesn't matter who the clapping is for—the applause could be for another gymnast who just stuck her uneven-bars landing—the sound still notches up my energy level.

• the crowds in atlanta •

Of course, it was impossible not to hear the crowds at the 1996 Olympics. They were so loud I thought my ears were going to burst. It was fantastic to have such an enthusiastic audience, and the crowd in Atlanta's Georgia Dome really supported the U.S. gymnastics team. There was constant background chanting and cheering, and it lifted all of us to a higher level of performance.

During my beam routine in the finals (my last chance for an individual medal), I had just done my press mount when a guy on the left side of the arena

Performing my beam routine at the 1996 Olympics. © *Dave Black 1998*

yelled, "Hey, buddy, turn your flash off!" I guess he was yelling at some man to stop using his flash so the light wouldn't distract me. The funny thing is, the entire Georgia Dome was filled with tons of flashes. Silver fireworks were exploding everywhere.

I'd never heard anyone yell something individually before that moment. I was really surprised, because I realized that I could lose my concentration at the Olympic Games. At the same time, it made me feel good that people wanted me to do well. I actually had to tell myself to stop thinking about that and concentrate on my next skill! Luckily I did, and the moment when I stuck my landing felt pretty incredible.

Whether it's in practice or at a meet, sticking your dismount—well, there's nothing better than that. It's a pretty tough thing to do because of momentum, and because there's little room for error. So to do something so perfectly, to hit the nail on the head, makes you feel great. Of course, winning the gold on the beam felt fantastic, too.

• the 1996 olympic competition, july 19 to august 4 •

It wasn't all gold medals for me at the 1996 Olympics. I had a lot of ups and downs. Winning the team gold was unbelievable, but the all-around and individual finals didn't go as well for me. I almost never step out of bounds on the floor, but I did during my floor routine for the all-around, and it knocked me out of medal contention. The individual finals two days later were tense. In the vault my steps were off and my hand slipped. I landed on my butt in front of millions of people. It was pretty disappointing because I'd made every vault in the warm-up, but it's what you do in competition that counts. Still, when I stepped up to the beam the crowd was behind me 110 percent. Their applause and energy made me even more determined to show the world what I could do.

I felt like I had something to prove to people at the Games, which is strange for me because usually I only focus on proving things to myself. But there had

The 1996 women's Olympic gymnastics team and coaches. *Courtesy of Shade Global*

been speculation that I was getting too old for the Olympics. For the last few years a lot of people had asked if I was going to retire and if I thought I'd passed my prime. After a while, comments like that started bothering me. Sometimes little things get into your mind and grow larger than they really are. I tried not to watch meets, listen to commentators, or read the many articles about me, but in 1996 I was aware of what some people were thinking. So to get out there and help win the team gold and then win an individual gold on the beam made me feel great!

I felt so much pride when I stepped onto the podium and heard the U.S. national anthem play and the crowd sing along. The idea that I was standing up there representing my country was overwhelming. The fact that people had rooted so hard for me to do well and that I was able to pull it off was just amazing. I started to think about all those hours my coaches had put in and how I was glad I hadn't let them down. I thought about my parents and the money they'd spent without reservation, their support, and the countless hours they'd driven me to and from the gym over the years. I just wanted to jump off the podium, run over to the stands, and hug them all—and thank them for giving me the opportunity to be there.

Last week one of my teammates from the 1996 Olympics and I were talking on the phone.

"Don't you want to feel it one more time?" she asked me.

"Are you kidding?" I asked. "Do I want to train eight hours a day, every day?"

But even though I laughed off her question, I knew exactly what she was talking about: the unbelievable rush of adrenaline and excitement that comes with competing in the Games, and that moment of standing on the podium before your country. That's something you want to last forever. . . .

• sometimes competition
isn't so thrilling •

There are times when even the excitement, the crowds, and personal desire can't give a gymnast the energy to excel in a competition. In 1993 I went to the World Championships in Birmingham, England. Despite feeling ill enough the day of the all-arounds to take ibuprofen, I won the gold. The night before the individual finals I was feeling a little better and excited to see what I could do the next day. I took ibuprofen for some minor aches, then went to sleep. I woke up in the middle of the night and realized I had made a major mistake.

My stomach had a terrible reaction to the ibuprofen. I was sick all night, and by morning I had stomach cramps and was dizzy. At competition time I was still feeling pretty rotten. I went anyway because it was the World Championships, and I counted on that rush of adrenaline I always get when I step onto the floor to help me through the meet. This time, though, not even the crowd's energy could get me going.

I fell three times during my beam routine. It was horrible, and each time I just kept thinking, *Get me out of here!* The first was on a layout—a flip in a straight body position—and I landed with my ribs on the beam. The second was on a simple skill. I didn't get hurt, and I don't remember the pain, just the disappointment of it all. I fell for the third time when I did my dismount. On my dismount, I overrotated and missed my landing. I was crushed, but I still had one more event to go. My next event was the floor, and I actually ended up winning that event. But that's because you can be a bit wobbly on floor and no one can really tell.

• what the public doesn't see •

Sometimes what the public thinks is the thrill of competition is totally different from what gymnasts see. It's hard to separate the reality of a situation from what the media portray. It's not that the press is trying to lie; it's just that they want a good, memorable story. But that doesn't mean it's completely true.

Kerri Strug's final vault in the team competition of the 1996 Olympics is a good example. Most people have seen the footage on television where Kerri does her first vault and hurts her ankle. Despite the injury, she went ahead and did a second one and landed it. That second vault took incredible tenacity and determination. Unfortunately, it was a double-edged sword. Kerri had to vault a second time in order to make it to the all-around finals . . . but because of that vault, her ankle was just too damaged for her to compete further. The media portrayed that second vault as an example of the thrill of competition. But for the rest of the team it was a mixed moment, because Kerri did that vault not knowing what we already did—that we'd won the team gold.

• being a good sport •

The one certainty about competition is that not everyone is going to win. But the most important thing is to be a good sport. No one likes to be around negative, mean-spirited people. Whether it's in competition or life in general, you have to have a sense of humor about yourself, learn from your mistakes, and try not to make excuses.

When I compete now in professional meets, I'm competing with a lot of my 1992 and 1996 Olympic teammates. We make a pact at the beginning of each meet to just have fun and show people how much we enjoy the sport. Of course, we all want to do well. But as long as we try, we're never disappointed with our performances and leave the arena with no regrets—regardless of who wins.

It's really the media that make up the rivalries between gymnasts. Kim Zmeskal and I are supposed to be huge rivals, but we're great friends! The stories are funny to us because we know they're not true. We've always rooted for each other in competitions and been proud of each other's accomplishments.

The truth is that none of my fellow American gymnasts is a poor sport. We've all been through the same things, put in the time, effort, and work, and so none of us can ever say that she deserved to do better than the others. When a competition ends, we know it's not always the best gymnast who wins, because we're all good. It's just that one of us had a great day and hit her routine at a certain time.

Sometimes people think gymnastics coaches are bad

Relaxing with Kim Zmeskal in 1997.

sports, since they see the coaches yell and gesture when they think scores are unfair and loudly disagree with the judges. But coaches in every sport do that—ever watch a pro basketball game? The bottom line is that they're doing their job in the most effective way. It's part of the game, and if there are hard feelings, they're usually left in the arena at the end of the day.

Gymnastics is a lot like life. You don't become an Elite gymnast by bickering and having a negative attitude; you have to be positive to get to that level. And anyone who excels in life—whether it's in business, school, friendships, or jobs—probably has a positive outlook and attitude to thank.

• the tour •

Me and my John Hancock Tour family.

The thrill of competition doesn't change for me, even when I'm on a tour such as the John Hancock Tour of World Gymnastics Champions. I can't even begin to say how much I loved the 1997 tour. I traveled with my best friends—my male and female 1992 and 1996 Olympic teammates—and Jessica Davis, Olympic rhythmic gymnast. We performed in major cities around the country, and though we flew to the first stop of each four-day weekend, once we were there we'd travel between places by bus. We had beds on the bus, TV rooms, a kitchen, and couches. A lot of times we didn't even sleep between cities—we'd stay up and talk, play games, and watch movies.

The show was *so* much fun. We did all of our routines to music—bars, beam, floor. We got to choose our own songs, and the music really gets the audience into the routines. Sometimes I had to remind myself to concentrate and not sing along in my head! Then there were the fans. Coming down to the floor during

Gymnasts in black . . . our "Men in Black" number on the 1997 tour was a real crowd-pleaser.

Our bus drivers are the best!

warm-up waving copies of *The Magnificent Seven* book and Wheaties boxes, cheering in the stands during the show: Their enthusiasm was contagious and I still got the adrenaline rush and that wave of excitement before I stepped onto the floor. And I still want to do just as well, for myself, my friends and coaches, and for the crowd.

Shannon's Advice: If there's one thing I've learned about competition over the years, it's that you should never compete with anyone but yourself. And since you may not top your best effort, you've got to learn from mistakes and disappointments and move on. Always remember to have a sense of humor and be positive. Life isn't just about gold medals. It's about what you learn along the way to success, and what you take from the experience.

Shannon's Golden Rule: God is your only coach. He directs your every move.

eating healthy

March 1995

Dear Diary,

I feel strong, motivated, and ready to try to make the 1996 Olympic women's gymnastics team. But there's no story in that. The story, I guess, is that I'm going to turn eighteen on March tenth.

It's all because of the McDonald's American Cup. I just competed in the competition in Seattle, Washington, last week, and I had an off day. My bar routine was okay, but my vaults weren't great. Then I slipped off the beam on a back handspring into a one-quarter twist. It wasn't even my hardest move. I'd just made a small miscalculation and all of a sudden I was on the floor! That mistake cost me a mandatory .5 deduction and put me in fourth place after the preliminaries.

Every gymnast has bad days. It wasn't because of my age, my fellow competitors' ages, or the fact that I've grown four inches and gained fifteen pounds since the 1992 Olympics. But that's what a lot of people want to point to. It's like they need an intricate explanation for what was simply a bad day.

Sometimes I wonder what people want me to do in order for them to accept the fact that an eighteen-year-old can still be a great gymnast. Stop growing, eating, and maturing? Even if I could, it wouldn't be healthy. And why does it always have to be a question of age and size?

I'm fortunate that Steve has kept me pretty sheltered throughout my career—I was never concerned about getting taller, hitting puberty, or gaining weight. I really didn't hear that this was a bad thing until I got older, and by then I'd gotten through most of it and was mature enough to handle all the talk. But if someone had told me before I got taller or gained weight that it was going to change everything— that I wasn't going to be as quick or fast or strong—then I would have started to believe it was true. And once you believe something like that, there's no way you can compete on the same level as before.

Steve never thought gaining height or weight was a bad thing. Of course he didn't want me to gain a ton of weight, but if I gained muscle, if I got taller, then obviously I was going to gain some weight. Steve had worked with college girls whose bodies had already developed into young women's, so the idea didn't scare him. He knew the college girls could still do all the big tricks. Since my coach had no fear about age or size, neither did I. And contrary to what some people think, my body's maturing has never affected my career. If anything, my increased height and weight give me more power!

• how i eat •

Last summer I ate a lot of pizza and Chinese food. I was traveling so much that it was just easier to order in. Every time I bought groceries, I had to leave town. I'd come home to spoiled food in the refrigerator. So I'd order take-out because it was late and I was too tired to cook. I ate fast food on the road, too, because there wasn't time for anything else. All in all, it wasn't the healthiest summer, but sometimes you just have to cut yourself some slack.

Usually I try to eat healthy. I'm a pretty picky eater, so it's not too hard. I don't like sauces, or anything I can't immediately recognize. And I especially dislike unappetizing-looking foods like cottage cheese! I've never actually tried cottage cheese, but it doesn't look like something I want to eat.

I eat a lot of little meals during the day, and when I snack it's on a piece of fruit, pretzels, or rice cakes (I love the caramel kind). One of my downfalls is sweets. My mom loves to bake, so whenever I go over to the house there are always pans of brownies and plates of cookies. I don't keep too many sweets in my apartment, but when I visit my parents I usually have to sample the baked goods! The key is not overdoing it.

I've become a discriminating shopper.

Here's a list of my typical daily meals. Of course, my list changes when I'm on the road or with friends. If someone brings over a pizza, I don't say, "Get that out of my apartment!" I love pizza!

1. Breakfast: Usually I have a plain cinnamon raisin bagel for breakfast and orange juice. Or I have a bowl of cereal with a banana and skim milk.
2. Lunch: If I'm in Oklahoma, I get frozen yogurt for lunch or a grilled-chicken salad. If I'm on the road, I eat a turkey sandwich with some fruit on the side.
3. Dinner: I love grilled chicken and rice. Until this year I didn't like most vegetables, but now I love steamed carrots, broccoli, cauliflower, and corn.

• dieting •

I can't see starving myself. Ever. First, if I don't eat, I get headaches. Second, if I don't fuel my body with the right stuff, I have no energy. I can't go to a six-hour practice without any food in my stomach. So anorexia is just plain out of the question. As for bulimia (which some people think a lot of gymnasts have), who likes to throw up? Anyone at the Elite level of gymnastics can tell you that you have to eat—to feed and fuel your body with good, healthy food in order to perform and succeed. And I don't know any successful coach who wouldn't agree. I learned good nutrition from my coaches. So if you think being thin is enough to succeed in gymnastics, you're wrong. You can't get out there and flip, twist, and tumble if you don't have the energy to train and perform. And a healthy lifestyle definitely doesn't include eating disorders.

There are *much* better ways to get your body in the shape you want. If you're

Doing lunch at Planet Hollywood.

having trouble with your weight, you should see a nutritionist. He or she can tell you what you need to do—how to cut fat where you need to or put it in where it's necessary. No-fat diets don't work, because your body needs fat. Only the right combination of eating and exercising will help you lose weight. Without exercise, even if you do lose weight, you could be losing muscle mass. The bottom line is that you have to have high self-esteem. Being thin won't make you feel any happier about yourself. That comes from inside, not outside. So if you're doing anything that's unhealthy, whether it's harmful dieting or an eating disorder, talk to your parents, a school counselor, minister, or family friend and get help before you do permanent damage to your body.

• nutrition •

I never consulted a nutritionist, but that's because I lived at home and between my coaches and my parents I learned how to eat right. As a kid I ate some fast food and desserts, but my mom also cooked a lot and she made sure to hit all the food groups. I ate whatever my sister and brother ate, and they weren't trying to be Olympic athletes.

Now there are so many health books out there telling you what to eat, when to eat it, and how to combine foods for a faster metabolism. There are all-meat diets, grapefruit diets, even cabbage-soup diets. I don't know much about any of them. I think you should stick to the basics. Drink a lot of water throughout the day: It fills you up, keeps you from getting dehydrated, and will help your body function better when you exercise. Use your common sense to tell you what's healthy.

When I can, I try to follow the Food Guide Pyramid: two or three servings per day of milk, yogurt, and cheese, two or three servings of meat, fish, eggs, and nuts, three to five servings of veggies, two to four servings of fruits, and six to eleven servings of breads, cereals, rice, and pasta, with things like fats and sweets at a bare minimum. Eating healthy takes some planning, and I can't say that I eat that way every day—but I know that when I do, my body responds better and I feel better because of it.

Eat the foods you like to eat—just make sure to keep the portions a reasonable size for your body. And remember that while eating low-fat is important, everyone needs some fat in their diet. But just because a box of cookies says "low-fat" doesn't mean you can eat the whole box in one sitting. That's not healthy in anyone's book!

• try but don't deny •

While the guidelines I've just presented are important, it's also important not to deny yourself anything. If you do, you'll just want it more.

After the 1996 Olympics I went to the Heisman Trophy dinner in New York with Amanda Borden. We had a lot of fun, but the food wasn't our favorite. Neither of us likes sauces, or food that's stuffed with meats and cheeses. However, we didn't want to be rude, so we ate as much as we felt comfortable with. By the time we got back to the hotel we were starving. There was a huge spread of desserts in the dining room, and when we saw the carrot cake we both went, "Oooh."

"I'll split it with you," I said.

"No, we can't do that," she replied. We headed to the elevators. "Okay, let's split it," we both said before the doors closed. We headed back to the dining room and shared a delicious slice of cake. I look at it this way—if I deny myself something I'm craving, I only end up wanting it more. Deprivation isn't the answer—moderation is.

I always try to make healthy eating a way of life, but I won't deprive myself. It's hard when I'm on the road. I eat at crazy times, sometimes really late at night. I frequently attend banquets—the meals are often quite good . . . but they aren't always as healthy as I'd prefer. And if I try only eating a little bit, then when the dessert is double chocolate cake or apple pie—well, before I know it the dessert is gone!

To try to get some control over my eating when I travel, I pack food—especially if I'm going to a country where I don't know what the food will be like. I also cut up carrot sticks or pack pretzels and rice cakes for the plane ride—that way I don't have to worry about what they serve on the flight. As for energy bars . . . they're good during com-

Me with Amanda Borden in the Big Apple, December 1997.

petition when you can't eat a huge meal. But there's no real substitute for a healthy, nutritious diet.

Even when I'm home, I watch what I eat when I go out. When my friends and

I go to the movies, I'll tote along a bag of dried fruit. If I don't, I'll eat popcorn and candy because it's there.

I'm trying to cook for myself as much as possible—that way I know exactly what I'm eating. There are a lot of ways to make things more healthy, like using low-sodium soy sauce, choosing light butter, and baking instead of frying. It doesn't take any more time to prepare—you just need to find good recipes. Here are some of my favorites:

Pasta Salad

One 1-pound box spiral macaroni
4 to 6 small tomatoes
3 green peppers
1 large red onion
2 or 3 stalks of celery
Black olives
Pepperoni (optional)
One 8-ounce bottle fat-free Italian salad dressing

Cook macaroni and dice vegetables. Mix together, along with a small amount of dressing to moisten. Chill for at least one hour. Just before serving, add rest of dressing. Serves 2 as a main dish, 4 as a side dish.

Chicken and Vegetable Stir-Fry

4 boneless, skinless chicken breasts

¼ cup orange or pineapple juice

2 teaspoons cornstarch

2 tablespoons soy sauce

½ teaspoon ground ginger

2 teaspoons vegetable or canola oil

1 cup snow peas

1 cup broccoli florets

2 medium-sized peppers (any color), cut into strips (about 2 cups)

½ cup diced green onion

2 cups white or brown rice, cooked

Rinse chicken and cut into strips. In small bowl mix juice, cornstarch, soy sauce, and ginger. In a wok or large skillet, heat vegetable oil over medium heat (add more oil if necessary during cooking). Add all vegetables, including onion, and stir-fry for 3 to 5 minutes, until they are crisp-tender. Remove from wok. Add chicken to wok and stir-fry for 4 minutes. Return vegetables to wok. Stir sauce and pour over chicken and vegetables, cooking and stirring for 2 minutes. Serve over the cooked rice. Makes 4 servings.

Baked Steak Fries

5 medium potatoes

2 tablespoons vegetable or canola oil

¼ teaspoon black pepper

¼ teaspoon garlic salt (or regular salt, if preferred)

½ teaspoon oregano

Scrub potatoes with vegetable brush. Do not remove skins. Cut into wedges. Soak the steak fries in cold water about 20 minutes. Remove steak fries from water and pat them dry. Place in a bowl and coat with the oil, pepper, salt, and oregano. Arrange steak fries in a single layer in a shallow, greased roasting pan or on a greased baking sheet. Bake at 400 degrees for 35 minutes, or until the steak fries are golden brown. Make sure to turn the steak fries at least once during the baking cycle.

Peanut Butter Cookies

1 stick ($\frac{1}{2}$ cup) butter or margarine, softened
$\frac{1}{2}$ cup granulated sugar
$\frac{1}{2}$ cup light brown sugar
1 large egg
$\frac{1}{2}$ teaspoon vanilla
$\frac{1}{2}$ cup creamy or crunchy peanut butter
1 cup all-purpose flour
1 teaspoon baking soda
$\frac{1}{8}$ teaspoon salt (optional)

Preheat oven to 375 degrees. Cream butter until fluffy. Add sugars gradually, mixing until creamy. Beat in egg and vanilla and mix well. Blend in peanut butter. In a separate bowl, mix together flour, baking soda, and salt. Add to peanut butter mixture. Mix thoroughly. Roll into 1-inch balls, roll balls in white sugar, and place on ungreased baking sheet. Press flat with fork dipped in flour. Bake for 12 to 14 minutes, or until the edges start to turn brown. Makes about 3 dozen cookies.

Those are just some of my favorites. I also love teriyaki chicken and chocolate chip cookies. Of course, it's not always possible to cook, or to control what you're eating and when. It's important not to beat yourself up over what you eat and just to do better the next time. There's no quick fix for staying fit, whether it's eating or exercising. Both take time and determination.

• food and fitness •

Exercise is really important for everyone—no matter what your level of intensity. Just get out there every day and do something. It can be walking, dancing, in-line skating, or taking an aerobics class. Regardless of which you choose, you'll feel more positive and happy because you exercised.

Not everyone thinks exercise is a great thing. Critics of gymnastics say that what we do is going to hurt us when we're older. I don't think any physical activity can be bad for you if you do it the right way and have the proper nutrition.

I've also been told that all the landings in practice and competition will eventually damage my knees and back. But I train so that my legs, stomach, and hamstrings are strong, and that way my knees and back are protected. I know a lot of people with bad backs and knees, but I've trained thousands of hours and mine are fine.

Everyone has some pain when they're in a competitive sport. The key is to work through it, and to know the point when you have to say, "This is enough for today." Sometimes that's hard to do. There have been times when Steve has had to tell me to sit out competitions. When my wrist was hurt before the 1996 Olympic trials, Steve made me sit out the meet. I wanted to compete so badly, but it wouldn't have been the right thing for my body, and I knew Steve had my best interests in mind. Taking that time off helped my wrist heal, and it made me a stronger gymnast for the Olympic Games.

Shannon's Advice: Drink tons of water. Eat lots of vegetables, especially green ones. Don't deprive yourself of anything, just eat in moderation. Always eat breakfast. Try to hit the major food groups every day. Don't try to follow a no-fat diet because you'll end up eating more. Snack as often as you want but eat healthy things.

Shannon's Golden Rule: You are perfect now, created in God's image and likeness.

discipline

September 1996

Dear Diary,

I can't let go of the bar. I'm not kidding. Every time I go to do one of my release moves on the uneven bars I can't let go! I haven't done bars the past few weeks, and now my timing is off, my arms are weak, and I can't do moves I should be able to do. I'm so frustrated. It's hard to even go to the gym and get on the bars at all. I really want to do it, and I don't understand why I can't make myself let go. It's time for me to leave for practice. I'll write more when I get back home.

I'm back. I spent practice going through drills I used to do eight years ago. Steve taught me a few new ones on the trampoline, too, and then we did timers on the bars. Timers are partial skills where you go up like you're going to do the skill but you don't release. Instead, you just picture the move in your head. After I could really visualize the skill, Steve worked me back up to letting go. It took a long time, but slowly I was ready to try. Once I did, I was fine. I didn't miss a beat and I didn't get hurt.

The whole experience reminded me of when I was first learning big skills. It took a lot of discipline to throw a move that scared me. And it took me a while to realize that I was making things harder than they actually were. Once I understood that Steve would never have me do anything that wasn't safe, and that he would spot me until I was ready, things got easier. But if I was really scared, that didn't work.

It's hard to make your body do something that your brain says is crazy. It always helps me if I can see a move in my head before I throw it. With new skills, I get glimpses, but until I can actually see myself doing them I have a tough time. I remember learning a rudi on the floor (a front somersault with one and a half twists).

One of my favorite photos. © *Garrison Photography—Edmond*

I couldn't see it for the longest time, and it took some serious determination to keep training until I finally got it down.

Gymnastics takes a lot of discipline—even after two Olympic Games! There are days when I have to force myself to go to the gym, reminding myself that hard work has paid off in the past, so it's going to pay off in the future.

Discipline is one of those things that's tough to maintain. It's hard to always be disciplined, no matter how well it pays off in the end. I try to give myself a little leeway, especially when things get crazy. Like with school. This summer I took some correspondence courses, and it was really tough to stay on top of the work. I even set my homework aside for two months because I was traveling so much. But five days after I returned home from my last tour, I signed up for a test. I knew if I signed up, I'd have to go in and take the exam. So I studied like crazy, crammed, and ended up doing pretty well. Sometimes I have to put myself in a situation I can't get out of to stay disciplined.

Right now I need to get some aerobic exercise. I don't really feel like going for a run, but I know I'll feel great when I'm done!

• what lies ahead •

My older sister, Tessa, always got A's in school. I used to follow her around and try to do everything she did. That included getting good grades. I grew up doing my homework in the car while my dad drove me to the gym. Finding quiet moments to study became my specialty. I'd read while I stretched out, memorize for tests while I waited for my ride to school, and cram for midterms during plane trips. If I couldn't get my homework done during the day, I'd stay up late, or get up before dawn to finish it.

After the 1992 Olympics I had a tutor on the John Hancock Tour. I was missing a lot of school, and I wanted to make sure I kept up with the work and graduated with my class. I'd go out and do my beam routine, then go back into the dressing room and take a math test. Then I'd go back out for my floor routine. I didn't do a lot of the group numbers, so I'd have time to study between routines. And if I wasn't taking tests or studying, I'd read a book or do whatever homework assignment was due. It took some determination to stay on top of things, but it was a way of life I'd grown up with, so it wasn't that hard.

School has never taken that much discipline for me. I understood it was important, and that attending college was a given. Both my parents went to college, so I always assumed I would go, too. A lot of athletes don't think about what lies ahead. They focus on goals and discipline within their sport, and not on what's going to happen after they're done. I always knew I had to have a plan, because I couldn't compete in gymnastics for the rest of my life. Some people might call that discipline, but I just call it being smart.

• look at the big picture •

My dad used to tell me that it didn't matter what grade I got in a class as long as I had learned something. I'd come home disappointed because I got a B on a chemistry test, and he'd say it wasn't a big deal (and he's a professor!). He'd ask me about the material on the test and I'd be able to answer all his questions. "So you forgot a few things for one hour," Dad would say, "but you just told me everything you were supposed to know. What's important is that you learned the material. Shannon, look at the big picture."

Life isn't as simple as a chemistry test. It's hard to buckle down and focus if you don't know what you're trying to accomplish. No one knows what's going to happen in their life today, tomorrow, or four years from now. It's important to have a plan, a big picture. You can deviate from it or change it completely, but it gives you something to work for.

I always assumed that by the time I was twenty I'd be going to college full-time, and that I'd graduate in the next couple of years. Then I'd apply to graduate schools. And so far, that's the plan. But I might not end up going to graduate school right away. Maybe I'll try my hand at commentating or acting. They're just other roads I can follow in the big picture of my life.

• choosing the right path •

Sometimes it's difficult to make the right decisions. I've learned from experience that if I really don't want to do something, I shouldn't. No matter how much hard work and discipline are involved, if your heart isn't in what you're doing, you won't do it well.

The 1995 McDonald's American Cup was one of my bigger mistakes. I'd just come off another meet and I was exhausted. Right after the competition, I was scheduled to fly to Mar del Plata, Argentina, to compete in the Pan American Games, a huge meet. I went into the McDonald's American Cup feeling like I shouldn't be there, and that I should have used the time to rest and train before the Pan American Games.

My attitude showed a lack of discipline, but sometimes that happens. Anyway, the McDonald's meet was a disaster. When I fell off during my beam routine, I was really disappointed, but I wasn't crushed. It was almost a relief, because I was just so tired. After I didn't make the finals I was upset, but I promised myself I would learn from the experience. My heart hadn't been in the competition, so I should've skipped it. I was upset, but I had to let it go so I could focus on the next meet.

The lesson I learned from the McDonald's American Cup came back to help me last year. Everyone really wanted me to go to the 1997 World Championships in Switzerland. I didn't want to, because I'd been to Worlds many times and won the all-around gold twice. Instead, I wanted to do the World University Games in Italy. No one understood why I'd pass up the World Championships for a slightly less prestigious meet. I tried to explain that the World University Games were something exciting and new for me because I'd never done them before. I knew if I went to Worlds and my heart wasn't in it, I wouldn't do well no matter

Pleasing the crowd is a thrill. *Courtesy of Shade Global*

how much I trained. But if I went to the World University Games, it wouldn't matter to me if I won, because I really wanted to be there. Choosing the World University Games over World Championships was the right decision for me. But if I hadn't made wrong decisions before, I might not have known that.

• discipline in the gym •

I won the all-around at the World University Games, but when I came back to Oklahoma it was time to start training again. Gymnasts are only as good as their last meet, so we can never kick back and rest on past accomplishments. After the 1992 Olympics, I was back in the gym three days later, ready to go! In order to get myself motivated to train after major competitions, I focus on learning new skills and routines and set my sights on the next competition.

When I'm injured it's especially hard to come to the gym. All the other gymnasts are there, training for a meet that's coming up and that I might not be able to compete in. While I do conditioning, running, stretching, or basic skills, they're flipping, twisting, and flying through the air. I don't know a gymnast who doesn't get really frustrated when she has to watch everyone else practice! When Steve's gymnasts are injured, he doesn't make us stay for a whole practice. We just come in for a few hours to stay fit. Otherwise, it gets really depressing because recovering from an injury is something we have no control over.

For me, the greatest thing about being disciplined is that it gives me control over my life. Even if I don't get the results I'm shooting for in school, gymnastics, or life in general, I know that I worked hard, was prepared, and tried my best. Discipline isn't a one-shot deal, anyway. It's not about whether you win one meet or get an A on a test. It's about what happens in the long run.

Shannon's Advice: Look at the big picture. Discipline isn't so much about hard work as it is about planning for your future. Make sure your heart is always tied to your goals, and remember that no one can buckle down twenty-four hours a day. Whatever you're trying to accomplish, don't forget to cut yourself some slack. Always do something because you have a passion for it.

Shannon's Golden Rule: Without honesty and truth, life has no substance.

faith

May 1992

Dear Diary,

This has been a really tough week. Dislocating my elbow after a fall from the uneven bars was rough. But harder still was making the decision to get it operated on and having the bone chip reattached with a screw. For some people it would've been a given—you get hurt, the doctor tells you what you need, you listen and have the operation. For me it was a little more complicated, because I'm a Christian Scientist.

It's hard for me to put into words exactly what my religion is about. Since my schedule is so crazy, I haven't been to church in a long time. Mostly, I just read a lot of material and talk to my mom (she's also a Christian Scientist) about our religion. What it comes down to is trying to be a good person. I think that's what all religions are about. And my faith in God has helped me a lot, because it gives me something to strive for and something to help me get through the tough times.

A lot of people think Christian Scientists don't believe in medicine. They think it's forbidden for us, but that's not true. Most Christian Scientists don't use medicine because they realize that they don't need it. If a Christian Scientist has a physical problem and feels the need to use medicine, it is certainly not prohibited.

When I dislocated my elbow and Steve took me to the hospital, I had a hard decision to make. I was worried that I might not really need the operation, and that maybe having it would be against my faith. I asked my parents what I should do, and Mom said it was my decision (Dad's not a Christian Scientist, he's a Baptist). I asked Mom to call a really good friend of ours who is a practitioner of our faith. A practitioner devotes all of his or her time to the ministry of Christian healing. I call this practitioner a lot when I'm traveling and having a difficult time with competition or personal issues. I wish I could tape everything she tells me because it just makes so much sense.

That night in the hospital, I talked to the practitioner about my concerns. "What if I don't really need this operation?" I asked. "What if having it is telling God I don't believe in His care and power? The Olympic trials are only six weeks away, and I know Steve and Dad think I should have the operation, but I'm not sure how my mom feels about it. I don't want to let anyone down."

The practitioner told me that if my dad and coach thought the operation was necessary, and if it was going to make them feel better and think that I'd heal faster, then it was okay to have it. "Just as long as you know who is really healing you," she said, "and you believe in God's power, then having the operation is fine."

I chose the operation. Someday, though, I want to be at the point where I can totally rely on my religion and push my fear aside. It's going to take a lot more time and studying, but it'll be worth the effort. God already gives me so much that I want to give Him back 100 percent of my faith and trust.

• have faith in something •

It's important to have faith in something. To me, it doesn't matter what religion you are. Having a constant in your life is unbelievably calming and helpful. To know there's a higher force that's always there (something you can grab hold of when you're having a bad day at school or wobbling on the beam) is such an important part of life. Faith can keep you company when you're alone and scared, and it can give you direction when you're lost. I don't know much about religion and I don't pretend to. But I believe in being a good person, and in the power, beauty, and kindness of God.

• praying •

I can't remember the last time I went to church. I spend most of my Sundays either in the gym or on a plane flying to a competition or event. But you don't have to physically go to church to pray, because it's not where you are, it's what you're thinking. I can pray at thirty thousand feet as my plane descends into an airport in Texas, or before I begin a floor routine in front of thirty thousand people.

For me, prayer isn't something that happens five minutes before I go to sleep. Prayer is in my mind at all times. Mainly, it's a lot of positive thoughts—knowing there's a higher being and that it's not all up to me, and realizing I can rely on God. I don't have to take everything on my shoulders, and He wouldn't want me to.

Prayer is a constant in my life, and it's helped me get through difficult times. I spend a lot of time traveling without my parents, and knowing I can talk to God really keeps me from being lonely. It also helps me stop worrying about my family when I'm away. When I'm at international competitions, I can't call my parents every day to see how my family is doing. I have no control over their lives or safety, so I pray to God that they stay healthy, happy, and safe. I trust in Him that He'll watch over them, and He does.

• prayer time •

There are times when I get so busy that my prayers slack off. Believe it or not, it's the national anthem that always reminds me about prayer. At every competition they play the anthem before the meet starts, and that's when I pray. I thank God for helping me to be there. I tell Him that I want to express Him in everything I do, and ask that He help everyone to have a safe competition and perform to the best of their abilities.

Praying calms me. When I feel like I'm in over my head and I'm scared about making decisions—especially the huge ones I had to make after the 1996 Olympics—I turn to God. It might be something as simple as "Should I even try acting because I might make a fool of myself, forget my lines, and look ridiculous?" Or as tough as whether to sign with a new agent, agree to a tour, or apply to graduate school. When I'm feeling overwhelmed, I remind myself that I need to think positively, that I'm where I am

During competition, I take some mental time for myself.

for a reason (I'm in my right place), and that God isn't going to present an opportunity to me that I can't handle. In the end, it calms me down and everything is okay.

Sometimes it's hard to put your total and complete trust in God. A good example is the individual finals at the 1996 Olympics, especially the beam finals on the last day of competition. I was sore and both mentally and physically tired from the team and all-around finals when I began the individual events. In addition, the Atlanta Olympics were very emotional for me. I wasn't sure if they were going to be my last international competition. Plus, they were being held in the United States and I didn't want to let down my family, my coaches, and the American public. Usually I can set my emotions aside—that's why people think I'm so stoic during meets. But I just had too many feelings to handle . . . an emotional overload.

I knew I was going to be crying tears of either joy or sadness during the individual competition. And the day be-

Going through my beam warm-up at the 1996 Olympics.
Photo by Gene Stafford

fore the beam finals, my tears came out of frustration and disappointment. I didn't feel like my faith had let me down; I just felt like I hadn't done as well as I should have.

By the time the beam finals came around, I was really nervous, and the beam requires total precision and balance. I just kept thinking that it was my last chance to win an individual medal, and maybe my last Olympic Games: I wanted to go out on a good note, but I'd had a not-so-great workout that morning. When I went to the arena to warm up I felt okay, but not fantastic. *Remember why you're here,* I told myself over and over again. *Remember what's important.* But nothing was calming me down. And then it was time for me to compete.

Peggy walked over and gave me last-minute corrections. As I walked toward the beam I said, *God, I'm in your hands. I'm going to do the very best I can. I know I wouldn't be here if I wasn't supposed to be—if I wasn't capable of doing this.* Suddenly I felt totally calm. I took a deep breath and did my press mount, and all of a sudden I was doing my beam routine and having fun. I was actually able to enjoy the Olympic finals! I won the gold, and that felt great. But knowing God had been with me felt even better.

• how religion helps •

Life doesn't always move along smoothly, and religion helps me to deal with the many bumps in the road. When I was in my mid-teens, I wasn't getting along great with my parents. It wasn't terrible or anything, but we had our share of fights and disagreements. I felt like they were getting too involved in my gymnastics career (which wasn't really true) and weren't giving me enough freedom. So I turned to religion to try to figure out the situation. Soon I was able to see that my parents were children of God, and that all they were doing was trying to help me. They just wanted the best for me, and to keep me safe and happy. I realized I was blowing the situation out of proportion, and once I could talk to them without anger, we sorted things out.

Religion helps me work with Steve, too. I pretty much put my life in his hands when I'm trying big skills. But what I finally realized is that I'm not putting my life in Steve's hands as much as I'm putting it in God's, because Steve is a child of God, too. And my coach would never want anything bad to happen to me or put me in a situation that would hurt me.

• mom and me •

My mom has a lot to do with my faith. She's never pushed religion on me. In fact, I can barely remember going to Sunday school, and once I began to practice on Sundays Mom never said a word or made me feel guilty. But my mom is pretty good at sensing what I need in my life, and in the 1980s, I was having a particularly tough time in gymnastics. I'd had several injuries, including a pulled hamstring, which took a long time to heal. And I had just started competing internationally, which brought me new pressures to handle. When my mom realized I was having a hard time going to the gym, she took me to see a lady friend of hers, the Christian Science practitioner who later helped me in the hospital. She made such good sense. Now she has become a good friend.

Sometimes when I'm worried about a competition, I call my practitioner for advice. The last time we talked, I was competing in a three-day professional meet. I felt really out of shape. I'd only worked out a few times the week before, and never three days in a row. Right before the meet I trained three days straight—the first day was great, the second day I was a little off, and the third day I was a disaster and could barely hang on to the uneven bars. "I'm never going to make it through the third day of competition," I told her. "What am I going to do?" She reminded me that God is my strength. She said it didn't matter if I'd taken a year off—if I needed to accomplish something and if it was the right thing for me to do, then I'd do just fine. Remembering her words during the competition really helped me out and kept me strong.

My mom is always there to keep me going, always there to give me new golden rules . . . and remind me of ones that helped a lot in the past. Here's a list of our favorites:

1. You are always in your right place. (This one helps when I'm in a foreign country—especially if I've had a hard workout or a bad day. I just tell myself I'm meant to be there.)
2. God is your only coach. He directs your every move. (When I'm afraid of trying a new skill, I remember that God is with me and He won't let me get hurt.)
3. Fear thou not; for I am with thee: be not dismayed; for I am thy

God: I will strengthen thee; yea I will help thee; yea I will uphold thee with the right hand of my righteousness. (I remember this one when I'm feeling tired and sore and need to know that God's behind me.)

4. God giveth power to the faint; and to them that have no might He increaseth strength. They that wait upon the Lord shall renew their strength, they shall run and not be weary.

5. What time I am afraid, I will trust in thee. (Another one for when I'm scared or feeling lonely.)

6. To those leaning on the sustaining infinite, today is big with blessings!

7. Resist evil and it will flee from you.

8. Whatever is your duty to do, you can do without harm to yourself.

9. Be ye therefore perfect as your Father in heaven is perfect. (This is a good one for me—it helps me to shoot for the top and try to be my best.)

10. With God all things are possible. (My favorite!)

• tests of faith •

When something terrible happens, it can make you question your faith. It's hard to accept that God wants us to experience pain and death, or that when we lose a loved one they were "in their right place." Looking at the big picture and trying to understand the good that comes out of a horrible situation is a big test of faith.

When the Oklahoma City bombing happened, our nation was devastated. I was at my house getting ready to go to school when I heard an enormous thunderclap. I looked up and all I saw was blue sky. I thought, *That's strange.* There wasn't a cloud in the sky. As soon as I got in the car I turned the radio on. Immediately a song was cut off by a special report that something was happening in downtown Oklahoma City. I turned from station to station, and they were reporting everything from a pipe exploding to a plane crashing into the federal building. It wasn't until later on that day at school that we learned someone had bombed the Alfred P. Murrah Federal Building in downtown Oklahoma City. The explosion had wounded or killed hundreds of adults and children.

It was a horrible, horrible thing. One explosion caused so much pain and suffering. I was struck by the devastation and moved by the fact that everyone who could help was out there doing their best to save lives and comfort the families and friends of the victims. People just gave and gave and gave, asking nothing in return. They just wanted to help.

Much later, I heard people from other cities say they were amazed by how Oklahomans worked together in the face of the disaster. The city stood still while people were being found in the rubble and rescued. There could have been mass looting and vandalism, but our crime rate went down to nearly zero.

The Oklahoma bombing was a tragedy—kids suddenly were without parents, and mothers and fathers lost their children in the blink of an eye. But if the bombing was going to happen anywhere in the United States, we were probably best equipped to handle it. Oklahomans have a friendliness, kindness, and compassion of spirit that are unrivaled. They opened their arms, their homes, and their hearts to all those who lost someone. And while it didn't bring loved ones back or ease the tremendous pain, it made the situation a little more bearable. I was really proud of the Oklahoma people and the way they reacted.

It's hard to look for the good in something like the bombing and harder still to see the big picture. Maybe it was the fact that an entire nation joined together for a moment in time—the state of Oklahoma was flooded with offers of help from around the country. It didn't matter what race they were, what religion, what social background—people just rolled up their sleeves and worked together. Their only motive was compassion.

The tragic death of Princess Diana isn't the same situation as the Oklahoma City bombing, but it's another case of having to look for the good in the midst of a terrible tragedy. I heard on the news that more money has been raised as a result of the princess's death than she could have raised in her entire life, hundreds of millions of dollars to support her charities. It's hard to find comfort, but I think Princess Diana would have been proud that even in death she's going to have an impact on millions of people who need her help.

I guess faith is about accepting both the good and the bad and still holding on to your belief. If you can do that, if you can lean on God in times of trouble and trust Him to guide you, you'll never be alone.

Shannon's Advice: Find something to believe in. Be a good person and look for the good in others. Try to find light in the darkness, and never forget that you're not alone. God watches over everyone and He loves us all.

Shannon's Golden Rule: Man and God are inseparable. God is love.

privacy

September 1996

Dear Diary,

   I just got home from the airport. I had a layover in Chicago, and as I was sitting by the gate I heard a little girl say, "Mommy, that's Shannon Miller." She couldn't have been more than five years old and she was so cute. She had little brown pigtails and Gap overalls with a pink flowered T-shirt. The mother looked over at me and said, "I don't think that's her, honey." I pretended that I hadn't heard her and went back to reading my book. In Oklahoma, it seems like everyone knows me and they're all a part of my family. But when I travel, I'm never surprised if someone doesn't recognize me. I have to admit that sometimes it's nice to be incognito for a few hours.

   The little girl decided her mother was wrong and walked over to me. She began reciting my scores from my last televised meet. It's amazing how much kids know! Another guy heard her and came over. "If you're really Shannon Miller," he said, "what was your score on the balance beam at the Olympic finals?"

   "I don't have a clue," I laughed. I really don't look at my scores! If he knew the real me, he'd know that I wouldn't know the answer to that. I don't think the guy believed me, because he just shook his head and walked away.

   "Is your hair real?" the little girl asked. Her mom seemed pretty embarrassed by that one. I ran my hands over my long, curly hair and chuckled. Kids always ask me that question because in competition I wear my hair in a tight bun so that it's out of the way. But when it's down, it's really fluffy and wild. "Yes, it's real," I told her.

   "I'm a gymnast, too," the little girl said. "And I'm gonna be in the Olympics just like you were, and be on TV and everything."

"Are you having fun in gymnastics right now?" I asked. She smiled and nodded. "Then that's all that matters."

I signed an autograph for the girl, then boarded the plane. As I waited for the flight attendant to go through her safety speech, I thought about the tour I'd just finished performing in and how much fun it'd been. It was such a great experience (after the tension of the Olympic Games) to travel with my teammates and perform routines in front of enthusiastic audiences.

On one of our stops, we met a group of young guys at a Hard Rock Cafe. They waited until all the gymnasts were done eating and were really polite about coming over and asking for our autographs. We took some pictures with them and then headed back to our hotel. When I went to Denver for Nationals, I saw them again, this time in the stands. They were seated about ten feet above the U.S. gymnasts, and when the halftime music came on, they stood up and began a choreographed routine to the song "YMCA." It was hysterical! Just to see people enjoying themselves so much at the competitions reminded me that having fun is what it's all about.

Talking to that little girl today and watching those guys make me feel really great about what I do. The idea that I'm giving people a little joy and opening their minds to gymnastics and all the things it can give back to them is extremely important to me. If it means that sometimes there's an article written about me that I don't like, or that a cameraman focuses on my tears after a difficult competition, it's not that big a deal. What I get out of what I do makes it all worthwhile.

I've got to go meet my friends at the movies. I'll write more later. . . .

• a private person •

It would be unrealistic for me to try to be a totally private person. Gymnastics puts me in the public eye. I'm on television a lot, and if I eventually want a career that's tied to gymnastics (commentating, appearances, and television work), I have to be seen.

It would be really silly for me to think that I could just have a "normal" life. And what does *normal* mean, anyway? Do normal people have television cameras following them as they walk around their college campus? Probably not, but if a film crew wants to film me at a speaking engagement or walking to my car after class, they can. It doesn't bother me, or hinder my work, training, or life.

For me, normal is a bit different from what other people might think, anyway. Normal is taking an exam and then flying to Europe for an international competition. It's biking with a

Fellow Olympian Carl Lewis and I were co–grand marshals of the 1997 Tournament of Roses Parade. *Courtesy of Tournament of Roses*

121

We had a super time in Pasadena.

friend and then traveling to California or Colorado for an endorsement, clinic, or banquet. It's going home on the weekends to have dinner with my family and then flying to New York to do David Letterman's show. Normal for me is what everyone else does plus a little spice.

Some people who are public figures try to separate their public and private lives. I don't do that because gymnastics is a part of me, just like being in the World Championships and being in the Olympics are pieces of who I am as a person. At the same time those experiences are not the only things in my life. I have family, school, and other goals. All those parts come together to make me who I am.

• my time •

I can't separate the gymnast from the girl, but there are times when I need a little breathing room. Sometimes it's just an hour watching television or reading a good book. This last year, it's been harder and harder to find time for myself. I've been flying all over the country, doing tons of appearances and autograph signings. I have to be a bit more creative in order to have some quiet time. When I need to be alone, I like driving by myself to the gym. It takes forty-five minutes and I can just chill out, listen to the radio, and think about whatever is on my mind. For almost an hour I don't have to answer questions or entertain anyone.

It's not that I don't like talking to fans. In fact, it's great—especially in Oklahoma, where everyone is so friendly. I love to sign autographs and pictures for fans, but if I'm in a hurry and I'm mentally ticking off the zillion things left to do on my list or trying to spend some private time with friends, I do get a little bit impatient. That's when I remind myself that the reason people want to talk to me is because of what I've accomplished in gymnastics, and that's a good thing. It's not going to last forever, so I have to enjoy it now.

I really love my life. The media attention and appearances are fantastic, and since the 1996 Games they've pretty much

Signing autographs at the Rose Parade.

123

Balancing beam or the rooftops of Manhattan—I never know where I'll be these days! © *1997 Frank Veronsky*

become my job. Still, I haven't put off my education. I want to push myself to continue with school but not to do so much that I end up sacrificing my grades. I'm taking nineteen hours this semester. I know all the attention I'm getting from the media is a once-in-a-lifetime opportunity. Gymnasts don't have a long life span of popularity, so I'm taking on everything I can right now. It's working out great, and I have the best of both worlds—an education and career opportunities.

• the hard part •

The hardest part for me about being a public figure is making friends. I meet tons of people all over the world and am with them for maybe two or three days tops. It's almost impossible to make really good friends in that amount of

Hanging out.

time. It's hard to even get comfortable talking with new people in only forty-eight hours. That's why most of my closest friends are the girls and guys from the John Hancock Tour. We've basically grown up together and they're my extended family. We compete and travel together, and we get to spend our spare time on the road doing fun stuff. I think best friends are the ones who have been through what you've been through. They understand where you're coming from and where you're going.

I do have some really good friends from school, and it's nice to hang out with people who don't have anything to do with gymnastics. But it's harder to make that kind of friend. A lot of times it's difficult for people to get past the celebrity part of what I do. Not that I think of myself necessarily as a celebrity, but if people see you on TV all the time, it's hard to get beyond that. Also, some people don't understand why my free time is so scarce, why I'm not around for birthdays and parties or to hang out and go to the movies on the weekend. They look at me and think, *Wow, you've given up an awful lot to be a gymnast.* I don't see it that way. I was never a huge partyer, so that's no loss. Plus, I've gotten to do so many amazing things—competitions, travel, appearances, publicity events, and television shows. And what I've gained in terms of life experiences far outweighs everything else.

One life experience I hadn't had much of until the '96 Olympics was dating. Because of my commitment to gymnastics, there hadn't been any time to deal with a relationship. Finally, though, I have time to date, and slowly I'm learning what I like and what I don't! A good sense of humor, kindness, honesty, intelligence, and strong morals are all really important to me.

• the right to privacy •

Sometimes things can go a little too far. I've always had photographers and cameras around, and I get recognized a lot, especially in Oklahoma. But I just go about my business and always try to be polite. I often get stopped in the mall or at the airport, but it's no big deal. It would be really hard to be so famous that you couldn't enjoy everyday things, like riding a bicycle or attending a football game. I'd feel like a prisoner if that happened.

I've heard the paparazzi say that celebrities get what they deserve, that they crave the attention when they're up-and-coming stars, yet once they're famous they want their privacy. There has to be a balance, and some mutual respect. And above all else, the media have to be responsible for writing the truth.

Last year, I had a disappointing experience with a member of the press. He was doing an interview about the John Hancock Tour of World Gymnastics Champions, and he joined all the girls in the show at the beginning of the tour.

We wear a variety of costumes on the John Hancock Tour.

The gymnasts had just met up, and we were still learning routines and getting used to the tour, the demanding schedule, and the bus trips.

The journalist spent a week with us. He rode our bus between cities, watched us practice and perform and get to know each other better. Every day we played outside, learned new routines, and basically had a great time. We were all really happy about the tour: the costumes, the music, and most of all the great routines we'd be performing in front of packed crowds. We spent a lot of nights on the bus playing games and watching movies . . . we were too excited to sleep!

When the article came out, I was really looking forward to reading it. But after a few lines, I felt a little sick to my stomach. The journalist had cut us to pieces. He put down the tour and the gymnasts, saying we didn't know how to have fun. It was so strange to have someone come into our lives, analyze us, and then walk away with a perception that was totally off. It hurt me that we'd opened ourselves up only to receive such negative, hurtful treatment. But, as someone who has lived most of her life in front of cameras and who has had hundreds of articles written about her, I feel the media have been quite fair in their portrayal of me. I have a good rapport with most of the journalists, photographers, and cameramen I've met, and it's always gratifying to see an article in a magazine or a TV feature about me that is accurate and honest. And for the most part, they are.

•my family •

One of my concerns when I started getting increased media attention was how it was going to affect my family. I never wanted my gymnastics career to hurt them in any way—for my goals to intrude upon their lives. Luckily, that never happened. If you ask them, my family will tell you that my success has been an extremely positive experience not only for me, but for them as well.

I've never sheltered my family from the press, because they've always been fine with it. My parents have had film crews from every major television network in their home. Mom and Dad are happy to grant interviews, and having film crews troop through the living room and set up camp in the kitchen has become a regular experience. In fact, it happens so often that some of the photographers and cameramen have become their friends! If at any time the media attention bothered them, my parents know that I wouldn't mind if they stopped granting interviews. The same goes for Tessa and Troy. As it is now, they don't spend much time talking with the press . . . it's not that they're against it, it's just that they have their own lives to handle. As for my fans, my family doesn't usually mind if a visit to the mall is interrupted by an eager fan, or if I stop to sign autographs or answer questions. They're proud of me and my accomplishments!

The sacrifices of time and of money that my family has made are exactly that. My entire family has been behind me all the way, and I want to protect them as much as I can. But as long as they're okay with the hoopla that's followed me for my entire gymnastics career, I'm okay, too. I'm just really grateful that they've been so patient about it all.

• the most-asked questions •

I love talking to young fans. It amazes me how knowledgeable so many of them are about my career. A lot of kids know how I placed in each individual event of a competition, my scores, and the skills in each routine. Usually they want to know when I got started (1982), what my favorite events are (bars and beam), and whether I'm going to compete in the 2000 Olympic Games (who knows?). But they also want to know different things, like the names of my dogs (Hunter and Dusty). If I have a boyfriend (not currently). What I do outside of the gym (see movies, hang out with friends, go to school, bike, and in-line skate). And whether I want

Dusty is a girl's best friend!

129

to compete in any other sports (I like to try everything and compete, but, except for gymnastics, not at the Olympic level).

I talk to a lot of mothers, too. They usually ask me about nutrition, coaches, and certain skills. As far as nutrition, I stress that it's really important for them to talk to their doctors or a nutritionist, because I'm not an expert.

I always answer the coaching question by explaining what I looked for in a coach: someone who is smart, safety-certified, knowledgeable, and a good person. Once you're sure you have a great coach for your kid, that's the person to ask help from on certain skills. It's hard for me to give that kind of information. First of all, I'm not a coach. And second of all, not everyone has the same problems with each skill. If a kid can't do a double back, it could be because of something small, like her block angle is off, or something like not having the right muscles developed to get off the floor. I tell moms to ask their coach, and to make sure to listen to what he or she says.

Mothers often detail their child's schedule and ask me whether their child is

I love talking with kids.

training too hard or not enough. Most of the time they're doing fine. But if a mom says her daughter is working out six hours a day, six days a week, and she's seven years old, that's probably not the greatest situation for the kid. I usually explain that when I was seven, I worked out about three times a week for three hours each practice. That makes the mom think, *Wow, Shannon was in the Olympics twice and that's all she worked out? Maybe my daughter doesn't need to practice this much right now.*

On the flip side, if a girl is only working out one hour a week and she's trying to make the national team, she'll probably need to put in a little more work. It all depends on what a gymnast is shooting for. If it's a college scholarship, that's different from competing in the Olympics. And the bottom line, as always, is that if a gymnast isn't having fun, she shouldn't be in the sport.

Shannon's Advice: Everyone needs some privacy now and then. But if you treat people with respect, usually you'll get the same treatment in return. And if you admire someone who's in the public eye, don't be afraid to let your feelings show, whether you take the time to write a letter or support the causes they stand for.

Shannon's Golden Rule: Charity is the bond of perfectness!

closing thoughts

• right now •

It's great to plan for the future, but enjoying the present is just as important. Right now I'm really happy. School is going well, and I'm having a fantastic time participating in the John Hancock Tour of World Gymnastics Champions each fall. Traveling and performing with my best friends is a lot of fun, and I'm just trying to enjoy this time in my life. My schedule is pretty hectic, and sometimes I overextend myself, but I wouldn't have it any other way. I love touring and doing clinics, exhibitions, and appearances. There are also a lot of professional gymnastics competitions, and those are great to compete in because the audiences are so appreciative.

I'm living for the moment, learning every day, and trying to stay true to what's important in life—family, friends, God, love, and a healthy dose of laughter.

• the future •

It's always hard to know what's around the next bend. I hope to continue the touring, clinics, and appearances, but a gymnast's fame is pretty short-lived, so I'm planning for the future, too. Of course, school is at the top of my list, and I hope I'll be done with my undergraduate degree in the next two years.

I'm also keeping my eyes open to different career paths. What little acting I've

132

done has been fun, and I'd like the chance to do some more. I also hope to begin sports commentating. I haven't had any formal training, but if an opportunity presents itself, I'd love to try it.

Sometimes it's hard to take hold of every opportunity that's available. Before the 1996 Olympics I was pretty involved with creating my own line of leotards (they've been out for about four years under the name S.M.). Training for the Games took all my time, and I had to step back from that work. I'd like to get more involved with the line again. The leotards went on sale in Europe last year and they're doing really well, so it'd be fun to try to further expand the line.

A lot of people still think that becoming a club owner or coach is part of my future plans. I don't see that happening. I've spent most of my life in the gym, and I still enjoy being there. If I made the gym my career for the rest of my life, though, I think I'd burn out. I can always get a job as a coach because of my experience, but I think I want to make a difference in the world in some other way.

• charities •

Right now I'm involved with two major charities. The first is the Red Ribbon Celebration for Drug Free Youth, whose purpose is to assist Oklahoma schools and communities in developing and/or improving healthy lifestyle programs for youth. I've been a spokesperson for the campaign in Oklahoma since 1992, but now that I have more time I'm going to be a national spokesperson. I'm really excited about my new role because I think it's so important to keep kids off drugs. Even in small towns, drug use has reached epidemic proportions, and kids need the tools to be able to say no to drugs and feel good about themselves. I hope I can be a part of that process.

133

The second charity I'm involved in is the Children's Miracle Network. The Network raises money for children's hospitals all over the United States and Canada, with 100 percent of donations kept in the community in which they were raised. Just being able to tour a hospital and know I've helped raise money for kids feels really great. Over the next few years, I'm hoping to expand my role with the Network and play an even larger part in helping to raise money for hospitals.

I think it's very important to give back to your community in some way. It can be as small as volunteering an hour a week in a literacy program, or as big as organizing food drives or raising money for worthy causes. The saying that giving is better than receiving is true. When you give, you get back ten times more appreciation, love, and thanks than when you receive.

• special thoughts •

I have been really blessed in my life. I thank God, my family, coaches, friends, and fans for the guidance, love, and support they've given me. My journey so far has been about so much more than fame and gold medals. I've learned how to be disciplined, motivated, and goal-oriented, and how to balance career, a public life and a private one, stress, and the ongoing job of taking care of myself both mentally and physically.

I'm still learning, and each day brings both opportunities and new challenges. I try to look for a silver lining in everything, and to remember that God wouldn't put a challenge before me that I couldn't face. Gymnastics has given me the confidence to know that I can do anything I set my mind to, and the opportunity to help other people realize their potential and goals.

Shannon's Advice: Follow your own dreams, not someone else's. Give more than you take. Live in the present and always strive to do your best. Have flexible goals and dreams. Don't ever forget that the most important thing in life is love.

Shannon's Golden Rule: With God, all things are possible.

if you want to know more

For more information about me and the charities I'm involved with . . .

My fan mail address:
SHANNON MILLER
P.O. BOX 5103
EDMOND, OKLAHOMA 73083-5103

To learn more about the Red Ribbon Celebration for Drug Free Youth, contact:
OKLAHOMA FEDERATION OF PARENTS FOR DRUG FREE YOUTH
410B EAST MAIN
JENKS, OKLAHOMA 74037
(918) 296-0404
FAX (918) 296-0505

To learn more about the Children's Miracle Network, contact:
CHILDREN'S MIRACLE NETWORK
4525 SOUTH 2300 EAST, SUITE 202
SALT LAKE CITY, UTAH 84117
(801) 278-8900
FAX (801) 277-8787
WWW.CMN.ORG

USA Gymnastics sets the rules and policies that govern gymnastics in the United States. For additional information on USA Gymnastics, visit its site on the World Wide Web at http://www.usa-gymnastics.org.